SECOND CHANCES WITH ST. NICK

VICKI HILTON

This book is for all those who have lost and regained someone very special in their life.

Second Chances with St. Nick began life as a short story in my early romance-writing days. It's a heartfelt tale of lost love and regret, but also one of hope, second chances, and enduring affection. Abbie and Nick's story holds a special place in my heart, and I hope you love it as much as I do.

Merry Christmas. V x

THANK-YOUS

To all those I've met on my writing journey and to all who've supported me, thank you from the bottom of my heart.

Special thanks, as always, to my critique partners and Beta readers. Josie, Heather, Jenna, Pepper, Sandi, Cathy and Lucy; you inspire me and your attention to detail and your support knows no bounds. You anchor me and keep me accountable and on track, spending hours of your own time helping me create better stories. Put simply, you are absolute superstars!

Thank you.

(Cover art - by me!)

1

HOMECOMING AND HEADACHES

I once read that coming home for Christmas was like getting a warm hug. I only hoped *my* warm hug didn't turn into a chokehold.

Were my thoughts a little dramatic? Well, yes. But returning to Pine Springs for the holidays wasn't my plan. I'd barely visited my hometown in years. That fact alone spoke volumes.

My fingertip whitened as I pressed the familiar doorbell. A muffled call of, "Coming!" came from somewhere within the house. I pictured Mom putting down whatever decoration she was fixing on the tree and rolling her eyes at the interruption. She always decorated the tree five days out from Christmas. You could set your calendar by her, and the results were usually spectacular. As Mom would say, the Cooper family did nothing by halves.

I exhaled, my breath curling up and around the evergreen garland hung high above. The lock clunked, and the door swung open.

My mom's perfectly made-up face greeted me, and she wore a smile as wide as Main Street. "Abigail! You made it! And only a day late."

My gut tugged as she wrapped her arms around me, her embrace threatening to crush the wind from my body. Her grin almost blinded me despite the mention of my lateness. Mom never let a dig go unsaid. She was lucky I came at all. I sat at the airport this morning, sipping my third coffee, wrestling with my decision to spend the holidays with my family.

But then, the real reason I came home appeared from behind Mom and my heart warmed.

Cissy.

"Abbie!" my cousin squealed, doing a little happy dance in the doorway. "Now I can *really* get married."

"What do you mean?" I giggled, extracting myself from Mom's arms.

"I mean, me getting hitched wouldn't be the same without you here." She reached out to hug me and I breathed in the apple scent of her hair. I smiled. There were *some* good things in Pine Springs.

She let me go, holding me at arm's length as if examining a new puppy or a fancy hat. "We dreamed-up my wedding years ago, remember? And, I know, I'm not marrying Justin Bieber like I planned, but who else is going to wear turquoise taffeta and keep me sane? I need you."

I widened my eyes. "Turquoise?"

Cissy chuckled and took my arm. "I'm only kidding. Come on inside. The whole family's here."

Oh, joy! I picked up my bag and plastered a grin on my face. Mom closed the door behind me, giving me a tight smile. The second I pulled up in the narrow hallway, she overtook me and ran her eyes over my face. Next, she gave me a head-to-toe-and-back-again inspection. "I'm glad to see you're eating well."

My face burned. What... the... actual? So I'd put on a few pounds since the split from my ex. I liked my new curves. A sour taste pooled in my throat. Cody would have had something to say about them, too. Not having to listen to his criticism any more suited me just fine. I'd declared myself a "Cody free zone," physically and emotionally. I'd forgotten how similar he and my mother could be.

I ran a hand along my thick braid, pulling off my winter hat.

A line appeared between Mom's brows. "You look good, but have you been getting enough sleep? You know, eye bags run in the family, right?"

I let out a sigh. Never a back-handed compliment free moment in the Cooper house. I spent most of my life being subjected to Mom's opinions and judgements. After years of criticism, I developed armor plating. Maybe it was time to shine it up.

With a sigh, I put my bag down on the floral rug. Cissy's fingers curled around mine. She turned to Mom. "Aunt Meg! That's just plain mean." My cousin turned to face me, a glow in her eyes. "You don't have eye bags. But if you did, I'd hope you had fun earning them. Now that you're single again, I can only imagine the hell you must be raising in California."

I smiled and pulled in the aroma of freshly baked something emanating from the kitchen. "Let's go say hi to everyone."

After countless hugs from my gorgeous dad and a quick chat with Cissy's parents about Christmas sweaters, she and I snuck into the kitchen. She busied herself with plating cookies, and I busied myself eating the M&M's Mom had baked into their tops.

Cissy sighed. "Don't look so sad. Your mom has always been a tough crowd. I guess it's her way of showing she cares?"

I gave a wry chuckle, tipping three blue-colored candies into my mouth. "You think?"

Maybe I was being harsh, but based on experience, I had a feeling that eye bags and extra curves were only the start of her onslaught.

Cissy grimaced, and I pushed up to sit on the shiny countertop with a smirk. Mom always hated when I did that. "I know she means well, but I won't lie. Living away from her has been blissful."

"Is that why you never visit? I haven't seen you in person for ages. Not since I stayed with you. What was it? Two years ago?"

My gut pulled. Sure, my mom was one reason I rarely came to Pine Springs, but how could I tell Cissy the other? All the feelings that'd kept me away for so long.

I turned to my cousin. Her head was tipped to one side as if I was about to drop some philosophical bombshell or, at the very least, a declaration on gingerbread's rightful place as a food group.

"Let's just say I have my reasons not to visit. But I'm glad I'm here now. I couldn't let you be the only one wearing taffeta at Christmas. Tell me, does your wedding dress look like a puffball?"

She grinned. "You know me too well. It'd give Marie Antoinette a run for her money." Cissy leaned in and picked a green M&M off the nearest cookie, popping it into her mouth. "I consider myself lucky that I'm important enough to lure you back home. And you never know, you could end up meeting someone wonderful at the wedding." Cissy wiggled her eyebrows at me. "Harry's been singing your praises to all his single friends."

Harry, her husband to be, was a nice guy, but I'd only met him once outside of mine and Cissy's weekly Zoom calls. I wasn't sure I should hand myself over to the bachelors of Pine Springs based on his say-so. Romance, even a quick fling, ranked at the very bottom of my list of priorities.

"I think I'll give them a miss."

Cissy rolled her eyes as if she was dealing with a tricky toddler. "Well, that's a shame. I'm sure there's more than a few eligible young men eager to 'make your acquaintance.'" She threw air quotes around the words and followed them with another grin. "I'd venture to say, the men of Pine Springs have missed you. You weren't voted homecoming queen for nothing."

I smiled and shook my head. Cissy was adorable.

"I'm not kidding," she said. "I'll bet Nick missed you. I've seen him around town a ton recently. You guys can't have talked in ages."

My stomach plummeted at the mention of his name. I reached to touch the small charm hanging around my neck on a gold chain. Nick's charm. The one he'd given me when I turned sixteen. As I pressed the small musical note to my chest, the skin on my palm prickled. Cissy didn't know the truth about what happened between me and Nick.

Of course, she knew that Nick and I were once best friends. How we were inseparable growing up. But she didn't know how our friendship changed and then ended. How I messed up any chance we had to be together.

Cissy had been young. She always just accepted that Nick and I were like two parts of the same whole. "Go one—go both," he'd say. And we stuck to our motto, right until we left senior high. I swallowed the lump in my throat.

I couldn't resist the opportunity to talk about him, though. I hadn't said his name out loud to another person in ten long years. "He never moved back to town after I left?"

Cissy shook her head, and my belly rolled.

There'd been a time when I knew Nick like I knew myself.

After what I'd done, he ran for the hills, and I never got the chance to explain how wrong I'd been the night I let him down.

"I always wondered what happened between the two of you. I thought you'd get married and have a billion kids."

In my girlhood dreams, I thought so too. But then, when he'd finally had the courage to admit how he felt about me, I'd run over his heart with a bulldozer.

"Hey, earth to Abbie!" Cissy's sing-song voice cut into my thoughts.

"Sorry, did you say something?"

"Only that I think your bridesmaid dress is going to knock everyone dead at the wedding. Maybe even Nick."

"Oh, please. Don't tell me it's a loud color. I don't want to stand out..." I pulled up short, processing her words. "Wait, what? Nick is coming to your wedding? You invited him?"

Cissy shrugged and moved to the sink to run herself a glass of water. "Well, my mom did. She ran into him and asked."

Blood sang in my ears, and I bunched my fingers to stop them from trembling. "What did he say? Does he know I'm in town?"

"I'm not sure, but he knows we're close, so I guess he'd figure out you're coming." She grinned at me like a proud mother hen. "He'll be glad to see you, and like I say, your dress is gorgeous. Slinky, even. You'll probably outshine me."

I slowly let out a breath. The dress was the least of my worries.

If I'd come back to Pine Springs thinking I could avoid my past, I was sorely mistaken.

And Nick? Nick and the way I'd left our friendship was a mistake I couldn't forget.

2

FAIRY LIGHTS AND FREEFALLS

The A-frame ladder creaked under me as I shifted position. Who knew hanging fairy lights could be so challenging? Dad always made it look easy.

Cissy wanted her wedding reception at our house. She'd picked a winter wonderland theme. The spaghetti of wires currently wound around my arms didn't bode well. So far, my efforts made the deck look less like a winter wonderland and more like Frosty the Snowman went rogue with a staple gun.

Working alone outside turned out to be nice, though. Mom and I were already on hair-triggers around each other. I bit my tongue for the most part. I didn't want any fights to upset my cousin's special day. She was the nearest thing I had to a sibling.

I stretched toward the eaves of the deck, the sturdiest-looking part of the roof. Just within reach, the spot provided the perfect anchor for my decorations. Mariah Carey belted out her Christmas hits on my air pods and I hummed along. Not that I could even vaguely hold a tune, but it was Christmas. Singing with Ms. Carey was obligatory.

Taking a breath, I leaned into the void, totally overextending. The ladder wobbled under my feet. Perhaps my gingerbread and M&M's assault last night had already taken effect on my waistline.

"Crap!" I hissed, waiting for the ladder to still. Once it did, I turned into my shoulder to nudge up the cuff of my woolen hat. It'd already descended to my brows, creating a light veil of hair across my eyes. With every movement, it slipped down another half inch.

The A-frame stabilized beneath me, and I toyed with the idea of climbing down and moving it closer to the eaves. It'd be the sensible thing to do, but with limited time before dark and the prospect of a lecture from Mom on the correct way to drape tinsel, I decided against it.

Instead, I stretched out again. Mariah sang her last melodious note, leaving me in silence, but no matter how hard I tried, I couldn't reach my target. With a grunt, I leaned as far as I dared, but according to gravity, I badly miscalculated my agility and my core strength.

As I overextended once more, the ladder wobbled anew. Only this time, far harder. Clamping my bottom lip between my teeth, I engaged whatever abs I had, just as a low, husky voice sounded from somewhere below.

"Be careful."

I sucked in a breath and jerked my head around. When I did, my beanie slipped even further over my nose, completely blocking my vision. Yay! Great time to come down with a case of yarn-blindness.

I didn't recognize the man's voice, exactly, but something about it—something about the way the speaker held onto his vowels—sparked a memory, and my heart ticked up a beat.

I moved my feet on the rung of the ladder to get my footing. Without a secure handhold on the A-frame, my knit-one-purl-one mask disoriented me. I had no idea where I was in space. With every movement, the wooden frame creaked louder. I must've looked like an idiot, playing a game of blind man's buff for one, but even my flailing arms couldn't save me.

The ladder wobbled wildly, and I shuffled on the top rung, letting out a whimper. "Oh, no..."

The millisecond those words left my mouth, the ladder gave one final lurch, and I pitched backward, leaving my heart and breath somewhere above me.

I sailed through the crisp air, sending a prayer to St. Joseph of Cupertino, patron saint of acrobats, for a soft landing. After what felt like forever, my body met a pair of arms, and I landed with an awkward thud against something solid and warm. An amazing aroma of cinnamon and pine tickled at my nose and the tiniest growl made my toes curl.

Whoever was down below had caught me, and as I lay cradled against hard muscles, a warm breath hit my cheek, and whispered words met my ear. "I've got you."

The intonation and the accent sent another tingle of recognition across the back of my neck. I had to see who'd broken my fall. Meet the man who owned that voice. Unable to use my fairy light-clad arms, I jerked my head, trying to nudge my hat back to its proper place. Having no luck, I shook my head instead, but I only drove the wool even lower.

"Hold still," the man said. After a heartbeat, the angle of my body shifted, and my feet kicked through thin air as my savior slowly lowered me to the deck. My boots met with solid wood, and I ran my hands over the chest I'd so soundly hit just seconds ago. Holy crap, it was hard. Big and hard and...

"You okay?" the man asked.

I nodded like a half-wit as his words dripped over me like warm honey. I was perfectly fine, but that didn't mean I wanted to move. To break the spell his proximity cast over me.

A throaty chuckle resonated in the air, and I bit my bottom lip. Warm hands grasped my shoulders as the man turned me around to face him.

"Let me help."

I shut my eyes tight. Light filtered through my closed eyelids and the touch of wool moved across my forehead.

"There," he said. "Hey, Abbie."

I sucked in a shuddering breath and steeled myself to open my lashes and meet my rescuer.

His face came into focus—high, sharp cheekbones and a thick beard hugging a square chin. A woolen hat sat low over his dark blond hair and his familiar hazel eyes, flecked with amber, raked over my face. They caught the light as the corner of his lips lifted a fraction.

"Nick?"

He didn't move, didn't say a word. Instead, he stared at me for the longest beat. Then a small furrow appeared between his brows and his hint of a smile disappeared. I steadied my breath and controlled the trembling of my fingers against his chest.

I blinked twice. My fingers against his chest?

Hold up. I was touching his chest!

Not just that. I was gripping onto him like someone had glued my hands to his flannel shirt. Like he was my last hope as I succumbed to quicksand.

With a sharp intake of breath, I dropped my arms to my sides and stepped away. My bunch of lights fell to the floor and heat fired on my cheeks. "What are you doing here?" And why did my voice sound so squeaky?

He moved his head back, nodding toward an old, gray truck parked in the driveway. An enormous bundle of holly lay tethered to the flatbed. Damn Mariah. Nick must have driven up while she noisily decided what she wanted for Christmas in my ears.

"Cissy ordered greenery."

I stared hard at him. Was that it? Three words? I didn't expect a big hug and a, "Welcome back. All is forgiven," but I didn't remember Nick being so quiet. So gruff. As I ran my gaze over his massive shoulders, my breath thinned. There was nothing familiar about the giant of a man standing before me.

Sure, Nick had been tall. But he'd also been on the skinny side. He played the violin growing up, preferring to practice than play sports. He hadn't grown the muscles that some boys had in school. But man, he'd made up for lost time.

"But why are *you* bringing holly?" I asked.

He shrugged and shoved his hands into the pockets of his jacket. "It grows on the mountain. That's where I live now."

My gaze moved to the gray and green range that formed the backdrop to the town of Pine Springs. Today, thick white clouds blanketed their peaks. "You live up there?"

I'm not sure why I was so surprised. From what Cissy said last night, no one had seen much of Nick lately. She said he kept himself to himself. I'd been out of town for so long, for all I knew, he could live in a cave with Yogi Bear.

Nick turned his head toward the mountains. Bronzed skin stretched over his corded neck, just above the collar of his shirt. I had the strangest urge to touch him. Feel his warmth under my fingertips.

A shiver ran over me, and I hugged my arms around my body.

"You're cold," he said, his eyes narrowing slightly.

Did he mean metaphorically or literally? Either would be accurate, I guess. But the status of my body temperature didn't matter. This was my first opportunity to speak to Nick in forever.

I brought my eyes to meet his, sending him a half smile. He didn't smile back, and my gut pulled. "Nick," I said, reaching out to touch his arm.

He drew back and opened his mouth to speak, but another voice cut through the chilly air.

"Nicholas!"

My shoulders sagged. Mom. I'd never have a chance to

speak in private with him now. My mother had a reputation for lacking tact or the ability to read an awkward social situation. Couldn't she see I was trying to apologize?

"It's lovely to see you after so long. And you brought the holly. I'm sure Abbie can give you a hand unloading it."

Nick shuffled on his feet, his boots scuffing the wood beneath us. "No need. I wouldn't want her to get prickly. Those leaves can sting."

I tightened my eyes, running them over his face.

"Well, no matter," Mom said. "I've just made some hot chocolate. Come in and have a cup. You look half frozen."

I smiled at Mom, but she didn't reciprocate. Apparently, she wasn't concerned with *my* body temperature. Just Nick's. I couldn't blame her. He had a fine body.

The wooden boards creaked under her feet, and Nick glanced at her before looking back at me. His face remained impassive. What was running through his head? I counted five breaths before he lowered his eyes.

"That'd be nice, Mrs. Cooper. Thank you," he said, his voice soft and lilting.

The apples of Mom's cheeks lifted high. If I didn't know better, I'd say he just proposed to her. Or she found out she won a lifetime supply of laundry detergent.

"Then come on in," she said, beckoning Nick to follow her.

He turned and walked toward the front door. As he moved, he left the scent of cinnamon and pine lingering in the air. I breathed him in, my gaze following the wall of his back as he dipped inside the house.

Nick was really here. In my family home. This could be the first time he'd visited in years, and we were about to sit down for a civil cup of hot chocolate in the kitchen.

Butterflies danced in my tummy. Deep down, hadn't I wanted to see him? Have the opportunity to say sorry. To find out what he'd been up to and if he'd missed me as much as I'd missed him?

I trailed Nick and Mom into the house, hoping they couldn't hear my heart racing. To me, it sounded as loud as a herd of reindeer hopped up on double espressos. Mom's tinkling laugh bit through the icy air, and the hair on the back of my neck prickled. I pushed out a breath. Something told me I was in for a little more than hot chocolate.

3

HOT CHOCOLATE AND HOME TRUTHS

I reached the kitchen. Mom fussed over the stove. She heated milk in a pan, and Nick leaned against the counter. He stared out the window, watching the squirrels picking nuts up from the bird table and taking them away to hide. I wrung my hands. Clearly, they had a better plan for winter than I did for my future.

I took a seat at the dining table and ran my hand over the checkered tablecloth. Mom chatted away to Nick about the wedding. He put on an admirable show of interest, nodding at the right times and smiling in the right places. He'd make a skilled politician. But every so often, I'd catch his eyes flicking in my direction and my heart would jump. They had the same intensity as I remembered. The same glow.

Only now could I take him in, and as I ran my eyes over his size—his bulk—I had to wonder how he'd turned himself into a Marvel superhero. He literally filled the room, and I swear he'd hit his head on the ceiling if he sneezed.

Mom put a cup of steaming chocolate in front of me and handed one to Nick. He blew over the top to cool it, then took a sip, licking his lips. I ran my tongue between my own. Damn, he'd turned out handsome.

Not that he hadn't been easy on the eyes when we were younger, but the man standing in the kitchen was a world away from my old friend.

Back when we grew up, the kids at school considered us nerds. Nick for his music and me for my brains. The two of us formed a kind of club. He had a quiet, theater kid vibe and I had train track braces and thick glasses. I shook my head and chuckled to myself. My classmates called me Bottle-top Abbie. There was nothing like a mean nickname to fill a kid with confidence.

My life changed the day I discovered contact lenses, and my braces came off. But my teen transformation from homely to homecoming queen hadn't just affected me.

I glanced at Nick again. Mom leaned on the counter next to him, looking like a tiny sparrow in comparison. Her laugh tinkled out into the quiet of the kitchen and I tuned back into their conversation.

"Well, it's nice to have her back," she said.

Did she mean me? Based on her welcome yesterday, I couldn't be sure.

"And it's lovely to see you, again," she continued, beaming at Nick. "Once your folks moved away, I didn't know if you'd ever come back to town."

"Your folks moved?" How did I not know this?

Nick's soft hazel eyes found mine, and he nodded. "A while back."

Mom folded her arms across her ample bosom. "Moving away from your hometown seems to be quite the thing to do. We've hardly seen Abbie in years."

I scoffed, taking a sip of my chocolate. "I call, Mom. Besides, Pine Springs is a long way from California. It's not as if I can just hop on a bus."

"California?" Nick's eyes searched my face.

He obviously hadn't taken the time to ask where I'd been all this time, either. Where I'd ended up. I couldn't hold his lack of interest against him, though. Hadn't I questioned if he lived in a cave with a cartoon bear?

"Well," said Mom, dragging a cloth over the already sparkling counter. "I suppose you've had other things to occupy your time. Parties. That fancy beach house of yours."

I rolled my eyes. "Which I don't live in, anymore."

She stopped her polishing and clutched the cloth to her chest. "Ah yes, that's right. Tell me, how is your ex? Such a nice man. Always so thoughtful."

I clamped my jaw tight. I'd call him more self-involved and narcissistic. I'd never told Mom too much about my life with Cody. She didn't know how bad our relationship became. The one time I'd complained about his asshole tendencies, she'd turned it around on me. Gave me a lecture on choosing unsuitable men.

She shook out her towel. "I could've told you that relationship wouldn't work out. He was a high-flyer and despite what you say, you've always been a small-town girl at heart. I don't know why you think life at the beach is better than being near your family and friends here at Pine Springs."

Um—should I use this cozy little "pep-talk" as exhibit A?

Mom turned to Nick. "What do you think?"

I widened my eyes. Oh Lord, please don't involve him. But, no, she carried on.

"I know you moved further out of town, too, but you've still stayed close to your roots. Should Abbie consider moving back home? Wouldn't *you* like to see more of her?"

A small furrow appeared between Nick's brows. With a barely audible sigh, he put his mug down on the counter, wiping his mouth with the back of his hand. "I'll go unload the holly."

A wound split open in my chest as I watched him walk out the door. Like someone had slammed an axe into my sternum. He hadn't wanted to answer her question.

But what should I expect? The moment I'd thrown away my glasses all those years ago, I'd undergone a transformation. Geek to a glowed-up beauty queen. Only, I hadn't taken my best friend—my first love—along for the ride.

I counted to ten before I rounded on my mom. "I'd rather you didn't discuss my love life in front of other people."

She clacked her tongue against her teeth. "It's only Nick. You've known each other forever. And anyway, he's probably not interested in your dramas." She shook out her cloth again, eyeing me steadily. "I never understood why you two didn't end up together. You were practically joined at the hip as kids, and I'd have bet my best china there was more going on when you got older."

"Mom, Nick was just a friend."

I'd told no one about the night we kissed—the night he asked me to the Snow Ball and said I was all he'd ever wanted.

Mom folded her towel and popped it on the counter. "Well, friends or not, he's turned into a fine-looking young man. Did you see his shoulders? I bet he could bench press a redwood. And it wouldn't take much more than a nice suit to clean him up. He'd make a handsome date for Cissy's wedding, wouldn't you say?"

"Mom!"

"What? Don't tell me you weren't thinking the same thing. I saw the way you looked at him. I'd have found him pleasing in my day, too. Nice and tall. Though he could lose the ponytail, and I don't know what he's thinking with that beard."

"Mom! Please." I mean, his sandy-colored beard was a bit of a shock, but now I'd had time to check it out close up, I found I didn't mind the idea. I'd describe my ex as preppy. Nick's "man of the mountains" vibe struck quite a contrast—in all the right ways.

"I'm just saying you could do worse. You and Nick have always been close. Who knows what could happen if you spent a little time together? And why is he still single, looking like that?" She pulled up short, placing her hands on her hips. "Is he still single?"

I had no idea. Cissy gave me no reason to believe he wasn't. But if I didn't even know where he lived, how would I know if he had a girlfriend, or a wife?

Mom didn't wait for an answer. "If I were you, I'd find out. Handsome young men are scarce, particularly ones with such fine manners."

The noise of a throat clearing sounded out behind me and I spun round in my chair to face the door. Nick stood there, eyes too wide for comfort, and pinned on me. Even underneath the beard, he clamped his jaw tight.

My face erupted into a firestorm. How much had he heard?

The room fell into silence. After four ticks of the kitchen clock, Nick spoke. "I've unloaded the holly onto the deck. I put some tarp over it, but you might want to get Mr. Cooper to hang it soon. A storm's heading our way in the next couple days."

Nick dusted off his large hands. Did I look at his ring finger? Yes. Yes, I did. And I couldn't deny the loosening of my shoulders when I saw it bare.

"Thank you, Nicholas." Mom smoothed the back of her hair as if she was getting ready to meet royalty. "Would you like to stay for dinner? I'm sure you and Abigail would love some time to catch up."

My gut rolled at her suggestion. If he'd heard our conversation, he'd think that both mom and I were angling for something more than a family dinner.

Nick shifted from foot to foot in the doorway, eyes bouncing about the room. "I... um..."

He glanced at me and the look in his eyes reminded me of a man pleading for his life at an execution.

"I'm sure Nick has things to do," I said.

Mom let out a little sniff. "Well, that's probably true. I hear around town you've been looking after your uncle. Is he on the mend now?"

With his bottom lip tethered between his teeth, Nick looked unsure—a little shy—and the sight took me back years. To the young boy I knew.

Finally, he nodded, reaching into his pocket and wedging his beanie onto his head. "Yes. And I need to get the truck back to him. Thanks for the hot chocolate, Mrs. Cooper. I appreciate it."

"You're welcome, Nicholas," Mom said. "Just remember, though, we'd love to see you at Cissy's wedding. You could even play your little fiddle."

I rolled my eyes internally. She didn't even consider checking with Cissy. If I knew my cousin, she'd have her day planned with military precision. "Nick played the violin, Mom." Still, anything would look small in his arms.

Nick lingered in the doorway. "I'll try, but I have to help my uncle with work."

"The wedding's the day after Christmas! I'm sure he can spare you. What do you say, Abbie? Don't you want Nick to come?"

His eyes darted to mine, and I swear his cheeks flushed.

All the moisture left my mouth. "I...well, um..." I cursed my sluggish brain. Perhaps I should add "eloquence under pressure" to my Christmas wish list.

He didn't even wait for my response. Instead, he looked at his feet and bustled out of the door without another word.

Mom gaped at him like a hungry baby bird, and she gave her head a quick shake. "Well. How rude. He couldn't have high-tailed it out of here any faster."

My stomach churned. Nick wasn't rude—more like terrified. I recognized his tight jaw. Some things never changed. And if not terrified, he must hate me—probably couldn't stand being in the same room. But how could I blame him? I hurt him. Maybe I should accept that Nick forgiving me was out of the question.

Despite the heat being turned up to the max, an icy shiver ran over me. After Cissy's wedding, I'd head back to the coast and restart my life. Find a new direction, a fresh purpose, and bury the uncomfortable feelings seeing Nick brought.

Taking a breath, I exhaled through pursed lips. It turned out I wasn't over my first love, but it was time to let him go. As I stared at the space he'd occupied in the doorway, my pulse jumped in my veins.

Maybe my heart hadn't gotten the memo.

4

SHOTS AND SHIVERS

I pushed open the door of The Timberline, Pine Springs' liveliest watering hole. A wall of warmth hit my cheeks, and the clamor of chatter and laughter washed over me. I ran my eyes over the dark interior with its pine paneling, the array of drink bottles stacked over the bar and the glow of pea-lights that reflected off the glass. I smiled. Some things in town never changed.

I hadn't been here in years. Dad used to bring us to eat and watch sports with him. But the smell of the old place was the same—beer, fries and wood.

I shrugged out of my thick jacket and pulled off my pink beret. Mom said its angora was too "California" for Pine Springs. But I spent my afternoon down in the next town, Pine Pass, trying on my bridesmaid's dress. I didn't want the ladies at the dressmakers to think I didn't know my satin from my silk. My denim from my damask. I needn't have worried. Cissy had picked out the most beautiful forest green dress for me. With my long red curls, I looked like a woodland goddess.

I ran my eyes over the wall of flannel-clad backs at the bar. I heard Cissy and her friends before I saw them. They huddled together, giggling over something in my cousin's hands. A piece of bright wrapping paper flew into the air, followed by a squeal of delight. The bachelorette celebrations had kicked off, then.

I stepped forward and tapped my cousin on the shoulder. She spun around, coming to a stop in front of me. She wielded a sparkly pink vibrator in her hand.

"Abbie!" she shrieked, her eyes bright and alive. "You came!"

I ran my eyes over her "weaponry." "Looks like you might do the same later."

Her eyes widened before she dissolved into giggles, launching at me with her arms outstretched. I was pleased to see her too, but it wasn't every day a tipsy woman bearing a magic wand manhandled me.

When she let go, I nodded toward her gift. "Maybe you should put that down. You'll be a married woman in a couple of days. You don't want folks to question Harry's skills, do you? Small towns love to gossip."

With another tinkling laugh, she handed her wand to a woman wearing a sparkly tiara. Cissy weaved an arm around my shoulders, her eyes bright and alive. "You look a little flushed, but I love that blue on you. You look like a sapphire on legs."

"Is that a good thing?" I asked. I'd picked out a high-neck blue dress with a cinched waist that skirted my thighs.

She winked at me. "I'd say so. My rules say your first drink has to be the same color as your outfit."

I curled a brow. "Blue?"

"Sure, hang on." Cissy threw me a thumbs up and disappeared back into the throng at the bar.

I folded my jacket over my arm and moved to hang it up on the pegs at the side of the room. As I did, the crowd's noise lulled momentarily, and the sound of a strumming guitar reached my ears. A guitar, and something else. Something high and haunting. A prickle ran over my shoulders, and I peeked around the corner.

There on the stage stood Nick, violin tucked under his chin.

His eyes were closed as he played along with the guitarist. He swayed a little as his notes soared and his face was a picture of pure concentration and intensity. He looked lost in the music.

His flannel shirt pulled open slightly at the top where he'd undone a few buttons. A light smattering of sandy hair peeped from beneath the fabric, and my breath faltered at the sight of him. His ponytail was untethered, and his hair brushed over his face as he moved to the music.

Nick's fingers danced over the strings like raindrops skipping on a windowsill. I pulled in a shallow breath. Did I imagine those same fingers gliding and dancing anywhere else? You bet I did. I was only human after all, and Nick was a thousand things I'd never imagined.

I bit my bottom lip as I watched, half hoping, half dreading that he'd see me. But as the song ended, I didn't have to wait long to find out.

At the end of his last note, Nick opened his eyes, finding me with laser precision. Like he'd known I'd be standing there. Something flashed within their hazel depths, and he pulled his violin from his shoulder, holding it against his chest.

With a shaky exhale, my gaze dropped to the instrument. A small yellow dot sat pressed on the wood. Butterflies stirred in my belly. It was the smiley face sticker I gave him when he passed his grade five exam. I stuck it on as we sat in his bedroom one afternoon, shoveling popcorn and listening to the radio.

I looked at Nick's face and pulled the corners of my lips into a little smile. A sudden warmth filled his eyes. Just enough to take my breath away and give me courage. With my heart hammering out a military march, I stepped down onto the dance floor and walked toward the stage.

I got to within an arm-span before he turned away and put his violin in its case on the side. The bulk of his shoulder met me like a solid wall, but I'd come this far. There was no way I'd turn back now.

"When did you get so good?" I asked, my voice high and quiet. "You have talented fingers."

Nick swung his head in my direction. One glorious, thick eyebrow lifted to the rafters. My cheeks heated. That sounded bad, right? "I mean, you've got skills."

His eyebrow didn't fall. Oh crap, did that sound even worse? I raked my eyes over his face. Even through his beard, I swear the corners of his lips trembled.

Nick huffed a breath and shrugged his glorious shoulders. "I had a lot of time to practice, Abbie."

His words burned into my chest. The pithy remark could have dissuaded me, but I wasn't about to give up. What I'd seen of him on our deck, here on the stage, and that look of heat he'd given me only a few seconds ago, had me wanting a whole lot more of him. I'd settle for small talk, if that's all he'd give me.

I cleared my throat and rolled one of my long curls through my fingers. "So, I wanted to apologize earlier. For my mom."

Nick turned to me and pushed out a throaty laugh. "She hasn't changed."

I shook my head. "Nope. She still thinks unsolicited advice is a love language."

Nick grinned—actually grinned—and the corners of his eyes crinkled. I fought the urge to run my fingers over the skin at his temple. I'd forgotten the power of his smile. With the scent of cinnamon and pine wrapping around me, I reached out and touched his arm through his flannel. The second I did, his eyes snapped down to my fingers and his shoulders lifted.

"And I know she can be nosey as all hell, but..."

That second, Cissy arrived with a tray of colorful drinks and a huge smile. "Two blue for you, and... oh! Nick!" She looked at the closed violin case on the side table. "That was you playing? Holy crap, you're good."

"Nick's had a lot of time to practice," I said, my voice far harsher than I expected. His eyes darted to mine, and a light shut off somewhere behind them. My belly thrummed and perspiration sprung to my top lip. Did he think I was laughing at him?

With an almost imperceptible growl, he turned away and picked up his case.

"Are you leaving?" Cissy asked. "The karaoke's about to start. You two could sing a duet. For old time's sake."

Nick came around to face us. "Karaoke isn't my style."

Unperturbed, Cissy pressed her tray toward him. "Then at least help us out with these silly drinks. I've already had too many, and I don't want to be drunk and in charge of my older and far hotter cousin."

A muscle ticked in Nick's jaw as he ran his gaze over the tray of drinks, then over at me. With the tiniest shake of his head, he picked up a shot glass filled with green liquid and slammed it down in one. After putting it back on the tray, he dragged the back of his hand over his lips, just like he'd done with the hot chocolate. Finally, he turned to face me. "Goodbye, Abbie."

With wide eyes, both Cissy and I watched him walk away. Her brows knitted together, pupils darting from side to side, mirroring the twisting of my gut.

"Man, he's changed," Cissy murmured. "I don't ever remember him being that grumpy."

I didn't either. And it hurt like hell. But I had a feeling the Nick I used to know was in there somewhere. I just hoped I got the chance to find him before I left town.

5

SLOW DANCES AND SWOON

Cissy and I stood at the bar. "Oh, my lord, I can't believe you made me do karaoke," I said.

She batted my arm with the back of her hand. "You weren't too bad."

I shook my head slowly. "I sounded like a cross between Ariana Grande and a chipmunk. Like I'd sucked in a balloon-full of helium before I took the stage."

Cissy giggled and cast her eyes over the bar. "You didn't shatter any glasses. That's a win, in my opinion."

Gripping the solid pine bar top, I tipped back yet another dubious-colored drink. I hadn't had so much fun in ages. Sure, the lyrics on the karaoke screen looked like a foreign language, and I hit my notes with the precision of a toddler finger-painting, but no one threw anything or walked out. Like Cissy said—it was a win.

As I put down my glass, the volume of the music amped up, and Cissy jumped off her bar stool, wiggling her hips to the beat. Within seconds, one of her friends put her arm through my cousin's and stole her away to dance.

I forced a smile, wrapping my fingers around my empty

glass. Glancing around, I didn't recognize anybody. There wasn't one familiar face.

A man's voice drawled behind me. "You about ready for another one of those, little lady?"

My belly rolled as the smell of stale tobacco assaulted my nostrils. I turned over my shoulder to see a dark-haired man wearing a lopsided smirk.

"No, thanks. I'm good," I said with a half-smile.

He stepped closer, resting his hand on the bar, so his arm was barely centimeters from my back. "You're too pretty to drink alone."

I tugged my brows together, turning around on my stool to face him. "I'm not drinking on my own. I'm with my friends."

His eyes flickered over to the dance floor and back. "Your friends aren't drinking. They're dancing. Want to join them? I could show you how to move."

A shudder ran through me as his beer-leaden breath hit me full on in the face. "Like I said, I'm good, thanks. Besides, I have two left feet. You'd end up with bruises on your toes."

The man looked me up and down, his teeth gripping his lip. "I'm sure there's many ways you could bruise me. My heart, my..."

"Ego?" I asked, twisting my lips. "Like I said, thanks, but no thanks."

A deep scowl scored into his forehead. "I was just trying to be nice. Trying to get you to smile."

I sucked in a breath, about to shut the man down once and for all. But as I did, someone stepped next to me and warm fingers curled around mine.

"That's my job."

I turned toward the voice, widening my eyes as the scent of cinnamon wrapped around me. I let out a small breath.

The second our eyes locked, my heart jumped.

With a squeeze of my hand, Nick brought his lips to my ear. "It's okay. I've got you."

My mind whipped back to the moment he'd caught my fall from the ladder. He'd said the same thing then. I didn't strictly need his help, but damn… with the jitters running through my body at Nick being so close, I'd take any assistance right now.

I smiled and Nick drew up to his full height beside me. I'd seen church steeples shorter than he looked right now.

Tobacco man blinked slowly as he looked up at Nick. "I didn't mean any harm. I just thought she might want to dance."

Nick tipped his head to one side. "And I appreciate you looking after my girl, but I think I've got it from here."

My old friend gently pulled my hand, guiding me off the stool. Drawing me closer, he led me onto the crowded dance floor. I looked around, spotting Cissy and her friends dancing to a tune I didn't know.

"You okay?" Nick asked, reclaiming my attention.

I nodded, about to thank him, but the tempo of the music dropped, and the floor cleared. I moved to join the departing crowd, but Nick held onto my hand, stopping me from leaving.

We stood frozen, staring at each other. My heart pummeled into my rib cage and my breath trembled in my throat. Eventually, he gave me a sad smile. "Would you dance with me, Abbie?"

I swallowed hard. My mind couldn't form words. Would I dance with Nick? Oh, hell yes. But I couldn't speak, I just nodded.

He closed his eyes for three of my heart beats before slipping his hand around my waist and pulling me close.

The millisecond our bodies met, mine came alive. Every nerve ending lit up with energy. Following Nick's lead, I weaved one hand around his back and brought the other to rest against his chest. The second I found his heartbeat, he brought his palm to cover my skin and rested his chin on the top of my head. I hadn't felt so alive in years.

Pressed so close against him, I dared to peek through my lashes. The man who'd offered me the drink had followed us and was staring onto the dance floor. After a few seconds, he moved back toward the bar. I turned my head away, looking up to study my first love.

I disagreed with Mom. A beard suited Nick. It didn't hide his cheekbones. Instead, it clung to them like ivy on a tree. His fair lashes gently flittered against his honey skin and my heart fairly melted at the smallest smile on his lips.

"Nick, I think we should talk."

He opened his eyes to meet mine. "I'm sorry, but I don't want to. I don't think we have much left to say to each other."

The bottom of my stomach dropped away, like someone pulled a trap door. "But I need to tell you why I..."

He shook his head. "No, you don't. I'd rather leave my heart intact this time." Nick let out a thick breath. "Has he gone? The man at the bar, I mean."

I faltered. I could lie—say the man was still watching—give Nick every reason to keep me in his embrace. But our movement would spin us around eventually, and he'd know I'd not told the truth. I nodded, blood ringing in my ears. "He's gone."

"Good." Nick's voice was low and gravelly.

I swallowed away a lump in my throat, about to ask him to stay, but the minute I opened my mouth, Nick spoke.

"Please. I mean it. I don't want to talk."

We locked eyes. The colored lights flooding the walls fought with the golden flecks in Nick's irises. He looked so sad. So devastatingly rugged and handsome. Against my better judgment, I nodded, and he pulled me back in close to his body.

I lay my ear against his chest and listened to the steady

pound of his heart through the solid wall of his pecs. I let out a tiny sigh. What I wouldn't give to be trapped here forever.

As if hearing my brain's chatter, Nick drew his hand across my back, resting his palm between my shoulder blades. His thumb moved softly from side to side as if committing the feel of me to memory.

We circled around to the music, moving slowly. With each step, each brush of our bodies, a pulse of energy nudged low in my belly. It took all my energy to not pull him into me. To resist the urge to press back into him. But all too soon, the music ended.

Nick and I slowly uncurled from each other, and I looked tentatively into his eyes. There was a glow there, but something else. Like emptiness or regret. My chest tugged.

After the longest beat, he took a breath. "Thank you for the dance. It meant a lot." The husky burr of his voice lingered in the air between us. Before I could reply, he took my face in his outsized palms and placed a soft kiss on my forehead. His lips stayed far longer than a friend's should, and my throat tightened.

After what felt like forever, he loosened his fingers on my cheeks, bringing his mouth to my ear. "Goodbye, Abbie," he said, before turning and walking away.

As I watched him make his way across the dance floor and out of my life, my heart skittered like a baby goat running on floorboards. I wrapped my arms around my body, trying to lock in his heat. He'd said goodbye once already tonight, but fate had brought him back to me.

I looked up into the rafters above, and a disco beat pulsed in the air once more. With a shake of my head, I sent a silent prayer to St Anthony, patron saint of lost people, asking him for one more chance to see Nick. I only hoped he could hear me above the noise.

6

SANCTUARY AND SNOWDRIFTS

I checked my watch for the hundredth time as the bus wound up the mountain. We'd been late setting off from Pine Pass. The bus company had taken time to put extra chains on the tires. I gazed out the window as the snowfall intensified. Delicate, shattered crystal patterns clung to the glass and gathered at the corners. All was dark outside, apart from the eerie white glow of the snow on the hills.

The lumpy seat dug into my back, and I closed my eyes as Bing Crosby's *White Christmas* reached me from the driver's radio. Tonight was Christmas Eve. I'd spent my afternoon down in Pine Pass again, shopping for a wedding gift for Cissy and picking up my bridesmaid's dress from the dressmaker. After their alterations, the gown fit me like a glove. I lifted the corners of my mouth. Dare I say the adjustments they'd made suited my "extra curves?"

I gave a sigh, wishing Nick could see me in the dress. After our slow dance last night, I'd thought of little else other than his arms around me, his lips at my ear, and the glow in his eyes. He said he didn't want to talk, and though his request left my belly churning, I couldn't argue or blame him. I just had to be content with the opportunity to hold him close.

Recalling the feel of his body next to mine, I closed my eyes. With the movement of the bus and the engine's throbbing, it felt like someone had tied weights to my lashes, and within minutes, I drifted into a light sleep.

After a time, muffled voices roused me. I woke up to see a group of bodies mingling in the snow outside the window. The inside of the bus had come to life, with the few passengers gathering their belongings and moving down the central aisle. With a furrowed brow, I grabbed my dress bag and followed a gray-haired lady, shuffling along the sticky floor. As I climbed down the steps, the cold bit into my jacket and the snow laid thick around my boots.

"What's going on?" I asked the driver.

He stood at the door, hands on his hips. "With all the snow, the bus ain't going nowhere tonight, miss. We'll have to stay here until they clear the road."

He gestured over his shoulder at a dimly lit inn nestled in the trees. The ornate sign bore the name, *The Pines Lodge*

I shook my head. "Stay here? Like overnight?"

"We have to. The drifts blocked the road both above and below us. Short of finding a flying sleigh and reindeer, I'd say we're snowed in."

I dropped my jaw. "But it's Christmas!"

He raised his brows. "Is it?" His brisk chuckle bit into the cold air between us.

Fair enough—it was a ridiculous observation.

"Don't worry. Betty from the inn will look after you. She'll find you a cozy room. I daresay we'll be on our way first thing tomorrow morning and you'll be home in time to open your stocking."

With a sigh, I followed the line of passengers trudging toward the front of the inn. Looking on the bright side, at least a night in the hotel would mean one less evening under Mom's scrutiny.

I stepped into the lodge, and after some hot chocolate and cookies from a cheery, red-cheeked woman, all other passengers and I settled into our assigned rooms. Mine was small and tidy, with a cloud-like double bed. But when I turned on the old TV for company, my own personal blizzard popped on the screen. The storm must have wiped out reception.

What the hell was I going to do for entertainment now? There was no internet signal this high on the pass. I wouldn't even get to watch cheesy Hallmark Christmas movies on Netflix.

Sighing, I rummaged through the cupboards, desperate to find anything to read besides the Bible on the nightstand. After flipping through a few empty drawers, I nearly sang the Hallelujah chorus when I found the well-stocked minibar cleverly tucked behind a paneled door.

I ran myself a hot bath, and after stripping off my clothes, slipped into the water. The collection of miniature liquors I'd lined up on the side of the tub quickly disappeared. After two bottles of whisky, two cheap vodkas, and one brandy, my head swam, and I closed my eyes as visions of Nick pressed close against me danced in my head. The memory of his fingers on my skin as he'd kissed my forehead.

The steady drip, drip, drip of the faucet matched my heartbeat as the water crept higher, warm against my chin. When it reached my bottom lip, I opened my eyes, grabbing the sides of the tub and sitting up.

What if I fell asleep and drowned in the bath? Quickly hauling myself out, I caught sight of my refection in the mirror. The heat of the water had turned me all puffy and my skin glowed a vivid pink.

I swallowed hard. What if I'd died and somebody discovered me like this? I didn't want to be a sensational headline in the *Pine Springs Press*. I could just imagine it now: "*Local Homecoming Queen Found Drowned, Drunk, and Very Pink in Hotel Bathtub.*" That would keep my old school friends gossiping for days and my mom hiding behind her net curtains.

Moving into the bedroom, I slipped into the soft, white robe I'd found in the wardrobe, curling it around my body before taking out my contacts.

I hadn't been called Bottle-top Abbie for nothing. I had appalling eyesight. To the point where I couldn't see much beyond the end of my nose. The optometrist declined referring me for laser surgery twice. But being blind as a bat had its upsides. Everybody looked a lot younger and prettier—like I viewed them through a Vaseline lens.

I dug into my bag and found my thick glasses, putting them in easy reach on the nightstand. Finally, I climbed onto the bed. Tugging the blankets up to my chin, I closed my eyes and sank into a boozy sleep.

7

LOST LOVES AND LAUNDRY CARTS

I woke with a start, my heart racing. The room was quiet and dark, lit only by the faint glow of moonlight on the snow outside. The eerie gleam reminded me of the plastic stars I'd stuck on my ceiling as a kid or the glow-in-the-dark slime I got stuck in my hair in fifth grade. But as I listened in the stillness, I swore I heard the distant sound of jingle bells. And a thumping noise, like someone was stomping around in heavy boots.

Craning my neck, I twisted my head to hear more. It sounded like the noise was coming from the room next door. Had Santa checked in for the night?

I chuckled to myself. How much had I drunk?

My throat burned as I swallowed. Yep, too much. I needed to rehydrate. Bleary-eyed and bleary headed, I tightened the robe at my waist, slipped off the bed, and crept out of my room in search of ice water and any news on the road conditions. I could picture Mom freaking out right about now, but despite my pounding head and wobbly legs, I made it to the door without bumping into anything sharp.

I stepped out into the dim hallway. As I glanced around, no

details snapped into focus—the surrounding walls remained a blur. On instinct, I reached up to the top of my head. Nothing. Just an unruly tangle of curls. The distant memory of my glasses laying folded on the nightstand had my gut plummeting right through the carpet.

I took a step backward, but my heart sank when the clunk of the door lock punctuated the air behind me. I sucked in a thin breath. Where did I put the key? With a racing pulse, I checked my pockets, coming up empty. Crap, crap, crap! Now I was half blind and helpless in an unfamiliar corridor. I hadn't bothered to take notice of my surroundings earlier. Only the snowdrifts and Nick consumed my thoughts.

I steadied my breath. Time to calm down, Abbie. Maybe someone at reception could let me back into my room. They'd have a master key for sure. But how the hell would I get down the stairs in one piece?

With a grimace, I reached out and groped my way along the wall, the slippery sheen of the wallpaper cool under my fingertips. Even without my optical limitations, I didn't have a reputation for being graceful. Hell, I'd failed all my ballet exams as a kid. Predictably, I found the only obstacle in my path—a pair of shoes. They tangled with my feet, taking them out from under me.

As I stumbled backward, my outstretched hand hit something solid. Before I could grip it, it slipped away under my weight. A groan of air left my body, and I went down with an unceremonious thump, butt meeting carpet.

Within a second, a wall of white engulfed me, and a shower of softness rained down. The smell of fresh laundry tickled my nostrils until, finally, pale silence surrounded me.

What the hell just happened?

I groped outward with both hands, finding taut material, like canvas. I pushed against it, but it sprang back. Okay, this was freaky, like being stuck in a tent with no door. I strained my ears for sound.

Apart from my racing breath, all I heard was a faint squeak, like a spinning wheel. The creaky whine reminded me of my old roller skates before Dad gave them a lick of oil every spring.

I widened my eyes. White fabric? Tent-like? The smell of laundry and squeaky wheels? There was only one ridiculous explanation, but it fit, considering I was in a hotel corridor. I'd locked myself out of my room, glasses-free, and flipped a laundry cart on top of me. Because, of course, if anyone was going to end up in this kind of mess, it would be me, right?

Drowning in sheets and who knew what else, reality hit me —laundry carts were heavy. There was no way I'd get out easily. What if someone found me like this? The Pine Springs Press would have a field day with that headline too!

I punched at the sides, gripping random laundry items in my fists. "Hello!" I called, my voice muffled by the fabric cocoon smothering me. "A little help, please?"

Suddenly, mercifully, as if St. Peter himself opened the pearly gates of heaven, a heavy clunk rang out and the white veil lifted.

I blinked into a sliver of light in front of me. A silhouetted figure—tall and broad—stood in what could only be an open doorway.

I swallowed. Hell. Saint Peter had hit the gym.

"Are you looking for somewhere to hang your pillowcase?"

The man's voice hit me like a jackhammer, and I inhaled a now-familiar scent of cinnamon and pine. My fingers loosened around the cotton in my hand. "Is that what I'm holding? I mean, I'd usually go for a stocking, but I was kind of low on options."

A low, growly chuckle rumbled through the air. It sounded like a bear enjoying a good tummy tickle. At the sound, a prickle crept up my neck and my hair raised, as if I was standing alone on the plains during a thunderstorm. "Nick?"

He leaned down and offered me a solid arm, helping me up as if I was a feather. The smell of wood smoke mingled with his cologne, and the heat of his body made its way through my robe. I couldn't see well, but I got the impression he was staring at me. Studying me, even. Under his gaze, my skin tingled.

Words came out of my mouth in a jumbled burst. "I… I'm… I'm in the next room." I pointed in the vague direction of my door. "I locked myself out, but my glasses are still inside." At his silence, I swallowed. "Remember how I can't see much without them?" I gave my shoulders a tiny shrug. "But at least I found the laundry cart… or… it found me."

My rescuer breathed out another low, throaty chuckle. In the gloom, I made out a smile playing on his lips. Well, if this wasn't Nick, it was good to know St. Peter appreciated humor. At least, when the time came, I could one-line my way into heaven.

Now fully upright, I steadied my balance. More laundry items fell away from my body as I wobbled against him. Thank goodness I still had a hold of his arm. And damn, what an arm it was. The outline of every single muscle made its way through the soft fabric of his sleeve. A shiver ran over my body.

"You must be freezing," he said. "Come in and warm up before we find you a spare key."

His voice caressed me again, but I hesitated on the threshold of his room. Following Nick inside probably wasn't the wisest move. Hadn't I spent most of the last twenty-four hours thinking about him and I locked tight together on the dance floor at The Timberline? And hadn't those thoughts turned decidedly murkier as I lay awake in bed last night? I could hear my mother's nagging voice in my head already.

"I don't care how well you know someone. Young ladies don't go

into men's hotel rooms without a damn good reason, or at least a chaperone."

Despite this not being Victorian England, she was probably right. But hell, I'd had enough of being told what to do. She and my ex could form their own club.

I squinted at Nick again, trying to make him out. Yes, I'd pictured him naked last night. Had all kinds of "non-old-best-friend-appropriate" thoughts, but I had to be practical. Tipsy and half-blind, I wouldn't get far on my own.

Instead of declining his invitation like a sane person, I swallowed hard, nodded and followed my first love into his room.

8

SECRETS AND SANTA

Nick's room was better lit than the corridor, and I could make out more of him—the unmistakable blond of his hair and the way he held his shoulders. I followed him inside, tightening my eyes at his broad back. Did he have on red velvet pants and a jacket? And why was there white fur trim at his neck and wrists?

He led me to a leather couch, and I sank into its cushions. I held my hands out toward the indistinct glow of a smoldering fire. Nick busied himself on the other side of the room. A clinking of glass and the soft glug of liquid made my lips bow. He had a mini-bar too; it seemed.

"Who did you have to bribe?" I asked, pointing at the hearth.

He huffed a laugh. "I have friends in high places." He handed me a glass of what smelled like brandy.

I closed my fingers around it, taking a sip. "Mom always told me I shouldn't take drinks from men who wear velvet. Or was it strangers? No matter. Either is probably good advice."

Nick gave a slow shake of his head. "And I shouldn't be

drinking on the job, but with this storm, I won't get any more deliveries done tonight."

I was about to ask him what he meant but was spectacularly side-tracked as he sat down beside me, stretching out his thick, muscular legs. The couch creaked as he settled.

This close, I could make out the hazel of his eyes. Sandy lashes fringed their edges. Time had lightly scored the bronzed skin of his forehead and as I leaned closer, the size of his body dwarfed me.

Electricity hung in the silence between us, and a hot flush moved through my body. Could he hear the hammering of my heart?

Nick tapped at the edge of his glass with his fingertips. Was he waiting for me to speak? He hadn't let me talk last night—let me apologize for my behavior all those years ago. But I had him like a captive audience now. I had to try again.

"Thank you for rescuing me. I always seem to get myself in the most ridiculous scrapes."

Nick took a sip of his drink. "I remember."

I paused, but he didn't say another word. Was he going to make me beg? I mean, I probably deserved it, but still. I shifted on the couch and wound my fingers through my hair.

Nick pulled in a breath. "What is it, Abbie?"

"What do you mean?"

"You keep looking at me."

Busted.

"I'm sorry, it's just without my glasses I can't see you clearly. But from what I can make out, you're dressed as Santa. I guess I didn't have you down as a man who wore fur or hung out with reindeer."

The apples of his cheeks lifted a touch, and I wished I had those glasses on to see his smile.

"Maybe I enjoy dressing up. I might've been heading out on a hot date with Mrs. Claus. Maybe the snow sidetracked me."

Why did the idea of him being on a hot date with anyone leave a nasty taste in my mouth? "Are you telling me you're married now, Nick?"

I aimed for humor, but his smile faded. "No. I'm not married."

His voice was so quiet; so gravelly. My toes curled. The sound of his breath filled the space between us. It came faster than it had a few seconds ago.

"Nick...?"

"No, Abbie."

I pulled myself up, tucking my legs under my body. "What do you mean, no?"

He took a mouthful of his brandy. "I told you last night. I don't want to revisit the past. There's nothing to be gained from it. We're two different people now."

I drew my brows tight. He wasn't wrong. I was a newly single narcissist survivor, and he had the build of a yeti. Not to mention he was hands down the handsomest man I'd seen in forever. But I needed to tell him what happened all those years ago and why. I needed him to hear me and even if he could never forgive me, I needed him to understand. To see I hadn't set out to hurt him.

I ran my eyes over his face. Though I couldn't see him in twenty-twenty, I could tell he'd locked his jaw tight and stared straight ahead. A log popped on the fire, throwing sparks into the hearth. The sudden flare of flames lit an idea in my mind. A way to get Nick to listen to me.

I reached for his arm, and he turned his head toward my hand.

"Look, I know you don't want to talk about... us. About what happened." I pushed a loose strand of hair behind my ear, gathering my thoughts. "And I don't blame you. I messed up, and I can't change that. But maybe we can try something else?"

Nick let out a long breath. "What do you mean?"

"How about this—we're strangers tonight. I'm just a girl called Abbie, stranded at a hotel on Christmas Eve, and you're..." I glanced at his Santa suit with a small smile. "You're St. Nick. And I need to ask you for something."

The silence between us gaped like a chasm, and my body fizzed. Like I'd tip into the void if he didn't respond.

Finally, gloriously, he replied. "I'm listening."

"Just for tonight, let's pretend we're not us. You don't have to be Nicholas, and I don't have to be... well, the girl who made the biggest mistake of her life."

He turned his body to face me, and I ran my fingers over his velvet sleeve.

"You want to role-play? You're serious?" he asked.

I mean, it could sound a little kinky in the wrong circles, but I'd try anything. If I played this right, I could get him to open up to me. I nodded. "Why not? Neither of us are going anywhere tonight."

After the longest beat, he lifted his eyes to mine and shifted on the leather. "Okay. You've got St. Nick's full attention. Tell me. What do you want for Christmas?"

I took a deep breath, my pulse bouncing somewhere between unhinged and completely chaotic. "To start over," I whispered. "I want to find my way back to an old friend. And maybe I need St. Nick's help to figure out how."

His chest rose and fell fast before he nodded. "Well, I guess I should ask if you've been a good girl this year."

The playfulness in his voice sent a tingle down my spine.

"Define good," I said. "It's all relative."

One of his brows shot up, and a smile settled on his mouth.

"I mean, I may have done a few naughty things." I took a sip of my drink. "May have upset a few people."

"How so?" he asked, his gaze pinning me to the leather.

And boy, if I didn't unload like I was on a psychiatrist's couch. I told him about my ex. The controlling, the undermining, the split and how, as a parting gift, I'd sliced up his designer wardrobe with a set of garden shears.

Nick shook his head. "I know that asshole. He made the naughty list this year. I left him a lump of coal in his stocking."

I smiled as Nick played along. Warmth bloomed in my chest—that familiar, easy feeling I only ever had with him.

With a sigh, he shook out his ponytail. In the shadows, I took in the sight of his tapered waist. I opened my mouth, about to ask him how he burned off all the cookies and milk the kids left, but before I could speak, he reached over and brushed a strand of hair from my face. His touch burned into me and the familiarity of the gesture set my pulse racing.

Letting out a slow breath, I ran my hand over the skin where his fingers had been. "I wasted too many years on my ex." My voice trembled and, as if sensing my sadness, Nick slipped an arm around the back of my shoulders. Without a second thought, I relaxed into him. The warmth of his body radiated through his jacket, caressing my neck. My heart swelled and a weird calm settled over me.

Nick felt like home.

"Tell me, where were you headed when the storm hit?" he asked. "I had to park my sleigh around the back."

I smiled again. My mind swam in the heat of the room, and I turned to him. "I'm home to see my folks. My cousin's getting married."

"Nice," he said. "Are the two of you close?"

I nodded. "We are. I mean, I haven't been back to town as much as I'd like, but she's visited me, and we speak often."

The leather couch creaked as Nick shifted. "You must be looking forward to spending time with your family."

My gut tugged. "Honestly? I hate being home again." I knocked back the last of my brandy. "Pinewood Springs, where I grew up, is too full of memories. You probably know the town. It has a lot of kids."

The corners of his mouth tipped up a little. "Good or bad memories?"

I leaned my head back against the couch. "Mostly good, but a few bad. Small town folks with small town minds—you know the drill. I couldn't wait to get away in the end."

Silence hung in the air between us, but Nick closed his hand over my shoulder, circling his thumb against the cotton of my robe. Goosebumps skittered across my skin and my breath quickened. Holy hell! He'd sent my senses into overdrive with one simple action. And I'd be lying if I didn't admit I imagined that thumb doing the same thing elsewhere.

Nick's voice dragged me out of my fantasy. "There must be something you liked about Pinewood Springs?"

I opened my mouth to answer but stopped short when he tipped his glass back to finish his drink. With the movement, the sleeve of his jacket fell away. I narrowed my eyes, straining to make out his forearm. Fair hair dusted each muscle, with a patchwork of symbols etched into his skin. As the marks danced in my astigmatism, I made out a trail of musical notes that disappeared up toward his bicep. My heart skipped. They matched the charm he'd given me. The one currently tucked away in my purse. I'd taken it off before my bath.

"You have tattoos?" I asked, fighting an overwhelming urge to touch his skin.

Nick pushed a breath out of his nose. "I do. Each one tells a story. But you didn't answer my question. I asked if there was anything you liked about Pinewood Springs."

As his thumb continued its hypnotic, circular motion, I stole a look at him from under my lashes. With his jaw clamped tight, I swear he barely took a breath. The room contracted around us, and I gripped my lip between my teeth. "Well, there *was* one good thing." I stared into the warmth of the fire. "There was Nicholas."

After a pause to rival the break between every Bridgerton season, he spoke. "Tell me about Nicholas."

As I gazed into the flames, a gentle smile settled onto my lips. "Nicholas was my friend. The only one I truly trusted. The one who knew me best. He understood what it was like to *be* me."

Nick tipped his head to the side. "What do you mean?"

I let out a little chuckle, lifting the corners of my lips higher. "According to everyone in school, the two of us were nerds. He played the violin, and I was plain and smart. The cooler kids hated us. I mean, *really* hated us."

Nick put his glass down on the table next to the couch. "You don't look like a 'nerd' now."

I nibbled on my lower lip, selecting my words. Working out how to tell him everything without making him run for the hills... again. After a few seconds, I spoke. "Well, as time passed, I grew prettier. Unfortunately, I grew weaker too, and I let Nicholas down."

I nestled into Nick's soothing warmth. He didn't pull away. Instead, his thumb continued its circles on my arm.

"After I ditched my glasses, I got a lot of attention from boys. They'd never noticed me in *that* way before, and man, it felt good to be seen. To be admired. Not laughed at."

Nick let out a tiny growl next to me. Not an angry noise. More like he was shifting the breath around his body. "So?" he prompted, his voice whisper quiet.

"So, it wasn't long until I'd morphed into one of the popular kids, while Nicholas stayed the same." I tightened my fingers around my glass. "The interest I got flattered me. I never had so many compliments. I craved the attention and the excitement. Having power like that was something so new to me."

"I can imagine," Nick murmured, his thumb still skimming my arm.

Could he, though? Could he really understand what drove

my stupid choices? I shook my head. "But it wasn't all good. I drifted away from my best friend. The one person who'd always been there for me. I should've been stronger, but we were so young, and I'd become so wrapped up in my world that I forgot who I was inside."

Nick stopped his thumb's slow journey around my shoulder. I swallowed hard. These words were the ones that I'd dreamed of saying a million times, but now I had the chance, they lodged firmly in my throat.

"Then one day, Nick came to see me."

After a long pause, he began his thumb's caress again.

"He told me he wanted to be more than friends. Said he loved me. Asked me to the Snowball with him." I turned to face Nick. "It's our town's big Christmas celebration. I promised I'd go, but when the night came, I let my ego take over. Instead of meeting Nick, I went to the ball with Pine Springs' star quarterback."

Nick let out a tiny breath next to me and invisible fingers grabbed at my gut, twisting hard.

"I know. It's bad," I said. "Nick still showed up for our date, but instead of meeting his oldest friend, he met ridicule." I fidgeted with the corner of my robe. "That same quarterback had bullied Nick for most of his school years. I'd chosen the one person who made him feel small and miserable."

Nick pushed out a wry laugh. "This Nick guy sounds like a loser."

My gut twisted again. "No. He was incredible. Beautiful. And I humiliated him."

On autopilot, I lifted my empty glass to my lips. Nick took it from me, our fingers touching for a tingling second. He put the glass down on the side. "Tell me, what did Nicholas do?"

I pulled my lips into a grimace. "He took off. Everyone was laughing at him. It was horrible." I turned to Nick, searching his face for some kind of reaction, but he just stared straight ahead, a vein pulsing in his temple.

"Next morning I tried to find him. His folks said he'd gone to stay with family in the mountains." I shook my head, trying to loosen the ropes of guilt that bound me all these years. "I never saw him in person again. I wish I could see him now."

Nick brought his thumb to a stop. "What would you say? If you saw him, I mean?"

I drew in a shaky breath, my chest tightening as the words hovered on the tip of my tongue. My pulse quickened and all the moisture left my mouth. "I'd tell him I'm sorry. That I should never have treated him so badly and," I paused, "I'd tell him I felt the same way. I've never loved anyone like I loved Nick."

He let out a gentle sigh next to me, and the brandy that lingered on his breath mingled in the air.

A tug of something inside drew me closer toward him. "I've left it too long. He probably hates me."

Nick gently picked up my hand, enveloping it with his own. His fingers curled around mine like bindweed—rough, powerful fingers—and my heart raced again. I ran my tongue over my lips. Every inch of his skin was a temptation, and my throat tightened at the thought of his hands touching my body, stroking the loneliness and tension away.

Nick spoke, breaking into my thoughts. His voice sounded lower, thicker than I remembered. "He could never hate you. You're too beautiful, inside and out. I think he'd remember all the good things. The special times you had together."

I rested my forehead on my palm. "Before I messed everything up, you mean?"

Nick shifted beside me, gently taking my wrist and placing my hand on the other one he already held.

"No. But I'm going to give you some advice from St. Nick. It's Christmas. You need to look forward, into the future, not backward to the past. The true spirit of the season is one of loving, sharing, and forgiving. You've shared your story with me tonight and I'm sure Nicholas would try to forgive you if he knew how you felt."

Nick paused, then turned to look into my eyes. He brought my knuckles to his lips.

"That only leaves us one thing to explore… if you'd like."

I widened my eyes, and my heart thumped in my ears, threatening to burst out of my chest.

He'd mentioned "loving…"

"Could I make Christmas better for you, Abbie?" he asked, his soft breath dancing over the back of my hand.

I stared into his eyes, blinking under their laser-like intensity. This man was so far from the shy Nick I remembered. The goofy guy I'd loved had gone, replaced by a quiet, confident rock of a man. Maybe my cruelty all those years ago changed him forever. But as I raked my eyes over his face, over the bulk of his body, my breath thinned. "What did you have in mind?"

One side of his lips peaked, and the air crackled between us. My fingertips itched to touch him—ached, even—and I leaned in, my gaze firmly on his mouth. I burned to kiss him. I needed to taste him and trace every tattoo on every inch of his skin.

Unweaving my fingers from Nick's, I reached out to brush his face, tentatively at first, but the delicious ache low down in my belly told me all I needed to know. Our breath came fast as I trailed a slow path along the beard at his jaw, coming to rest at the back of his hard neck. I gently drew him in, desperate to bring his lips closer to mine. "Nick," I whispered.

He shook his head slowly, his eyes alive with hunger. "Remember, tonight we're strangers."

I bobbed my head once, and a smile split his face. "Then come and sit on my knee and tell me what you'd like for Christmas."

My whole body fizzed. I didn't need to be asked twice. Reaching over, he pulled me easily onto his lap, and I brought my mouth to his. Gently at first, I savored his softness. He smelled sweet and warm, and I had to wonder why I'd stayed away so long. Why had I ever been so stupid as to let him go?

I ran my tongue along his bottom lip and Nick opened his mouth to me. Our tongues met and circled, slowly at first, but soon we moved together faster, urgently. His beard scraped against my lips and with the pull of his heat, I hung on for dear life.

He tasted delicious, all cinnamon and brandy. My brain swam in a sea of sensation. As we tangled tighter, Nick circled my waist with his large hands, his thumbs working my skin through my robe. As they crept up my ribs, my nipples pebbled against the soft cotton and an ache low down pleaded silently for him to touch me.

My body wanted Nick. Needed him. Plain and simple.

I rocked my hips into his, finding his hardness. Moving my lips to his neck, I dragged my fingers over his solid shoulders and down his chest.

A guttural groan escaped his mouth and at his deep growl, my core ached even more. Emboldened, I kissed him harder—deeper—until he shifted under me.

"Stop," he hissed, pulling away.

A burn ripped through my chest. Had I done some damage? Had I broken him? Did he have regrets? I searched his face for a clue.

"Buckle," he panted.

"Wait, what?"

"My buckle. Hold on."

As easily as he'd lifted me on, Nick moved me off his lap and back onto the couch. A bubble of delight sprang in my chest. Unlike some, he didn't seem to have a problem with my "extra curves."

With a groan, he stood, towering over me. I couldn't tell if he was looking my way, but when he reached down and undid his belt, I felt the burn of his eyes searing me. The leather slapped as he pulled it free, and my cheeks flamed when he dropped it to the carpet. If only I could see clearly! The hazy blur of being half-blind was pure torture.

Once he freed his belt, he kicked off his heavy boots and brought his fingers to the buttons of his jacket. "It's getting a little hot in here. Do you mind?" He undid the first, then the second, then paused.

At the delay, I bit the side of my lip. "Oh, I don't mind at all," I said, desperate for him to continue his Christmas strip show.

Nick moved through his buttons, one by one, taking his time, before finally shedding his jacket. He laid it over the back of the couch. Even with my unfocused vision, his body was magnificent. Strong and firm, and...

"Holy hell, you look incredible." My voice came out raspy and thick with lust. Maybe I should have been subtler, but honestly, who had the time?

He chuckled. "I work hard."

With a low grunt, he nudged the table away with one thick calf, before dropping to his knees in front of me. He reached out his hands, taking mine, his eyes full of fire. This close, I could make out his tattoos better. They covered his chest and arms like he wore an inky jacket.

"I think you've got some choices to make," he said.

My stomach dropped. Was he about to go all "deep and meaningful" on me? It was all I'd wanted earlier, but couldn't we just play pretend a little longer?

"I do?"

Nick nodded, a smile spreading across his face. "Yeah, you do. I'm here for you, but you need to decide if you want *me* tonight."

I swallowed, a burn spreading up through my chest. "Want

what?" I squeaked. I mean, I'd take whatever he offered right now, but a little clarification wouldn't go amiss.

Nick let go of my hands and ran his palms up my thighs, nudging my robe a little higher. "Santa might have a gift for you."

He threw me a wink, and I had to giggle. It was like all the barriers; all the regret and guilt of the last ten years had fallen away. Even after all I'd done, Nick was here with me. *For* me. Offering me anything I desired.

I took his face in my hands. "I want you. More than you know. But I'm not sure I'm built for leather."

Nick ran his eyes over the couch then leaned down and kissed the inside of my knee. The touch of his lips and the scrape of his beard sent a shiver up my thigh, and I sucked in a breath.

"On the bed, then?" he asked.

I gave him a smile and shrugged. "If you're offering."

With a throaty chuckle, he got to his feet and bent to scoop me up. Held tight against his warm skin, I brought my lips to his chest. Even after all the years I'd known him, I never imagined that one day I'd kiss his naked skin. Not like this. With a sigh, I threaded my arms around his neck, and he leaned down to kiss the top of my head.

Nick carried me to the bed and laid me down gently. The thrum of my heartbeat echoed in my ears as he joined me on the mattress. Within a second, he pulled me to rest on top of him. All the breath left my lungs at the hardness of his body beneath me, his sheer size. With his enormous torso, I'd need supplemental oxygen to survive the night.

Fully intending to discover every inch of him, I leaned over, pressing my mouth to his chest. With my fingers, then with my tongue, I traced the outline of his tattoos—exploring his skin like braille. He felt so good under my hands, hot and hard.

When he tipped his head in pure delight, I couldn't contain my smile.

"I want you, too," he whispered, tangling his fingers in the hair at the nape of my neck. My heart skipped a little at his words, and the heat at my core ignited into a full-on blaze.

I nipped at his skin with my teeth, gently teasing. He slowly drew his hands down my back. Cupping my buttocks, he pulled me into him, fierce and hard.

A bolt of pure pleasure swept through my body. At this rate, I'd be coming like a freight train before we even started. I had to slow things down. Take a breath. I wanted to enjoy Nick. Lock our kisses away in my memory banks for lonely nights when I returned to California. There was no need to rush.

With superhuman restraint, I sat up, resting my hands on his abs. "I have to ask. Do you meet women in hotels often?" My voice was tight and thin.

A flash of teeth revealed his smile. "You know what they say about Santa only coming once a year? Christmas Eve is the only time I get to play. I need to make the most of my night."

I grinned and shook my head slowly, running my nails over the indentations of the muscles on his stomach. Across the planes of his chest. Nick pushed up with one arm to join me. With his other hand, he moved my robe aside, exposing one of my breasts. Leaning in, he took my nipple into his mouth, biting me gently. Not hard, but playful. When I gasped, he pulled me back down on top of him and as the two of us melted into the mattress, I dug my nails into his shoulders.

With a growl, he arced against me. I flicked my eyebrows and reached down to work on his zipper. Nick shifted, giving me room to move. I nudged the heavy velvet down, and a glorious wave of wantonness swept over me. Pressed so close against him now—with his breath hot on my skin, I felt like a goddess. Divine, powerful, and beautiful.

Slowly, I released him from his pants and took his solid length in my hand.

"Abbie," he groaned as I worked my hand along his length, teasing him. Giving him everything, then taking it away, again and again, until his breath came in heavy gasps.

"I need to be inside you," he said, his voice hoarse and hard. "Do you want that?"

"Yes," I said, trying in vain to control my breathing. I was a mess, and only the feel of Nick, and his arms wrapped around me, would put me back together.

Whispering words I couldn't even process, he turned me over, brushing his lips over mine. "I promise I'll be right back."

I lay alone in the gloom, tugging my robe around my body. Nick reached for something beside the bed, and I pulled in the smell of smoke from the fire. After a long beat, a tearing of foil mixed with our fast breath. Thank goodness he'd come armed and dangerous. I didn't like his chances of rustling up a condom at the hotel reception.

After a long beat, he rolled back toward me. He'd kicked off his trousers, and his skin glowed in the firelight. As he settled at my side, he rested an elbow on the mattress, head in his palm.

I glanced down. "Wow, you really *do* have everything you need in your sack."

He grinned, moving his lips to behind my ear. "I need to be ready for action. You never know who you might meet by the chimney." With a chuckle, he kissed the tip of my nose.

Nick took my hand, cradling it in his, and kissed my mouth softly. Slowly. Like he was savoring my taste. We were close enough I could focus on his hazel eyes and as they met with mine, a burn of embers filled them. Staying close, Nick pushed my robe open. His fingers trembled as he peeled it away.

He took me in, his breath catching as I smiled. This beautiful man wanted me—desired me. He brushed a strand of hair behind my ear, trailing his fingers over my throat. Under his touch, my skin prickled with a thousand goosebumps. The heat of the fire and the hunger in his eyes mixed with the chill in the air, setting every nerve on high alert.

"You're so beautiful," he whispered as he traced his fingers from my collarbone, across my stomach, and then down, further still. The muscles of my belly jumped at his touch, like jittery addicts gone cold turkey as he passed over them—lower and lower. By the time he reached the apex of my thighs I was a mess. He gently nudged my legs apart and it was all I could do to hold myself together.

In one simple move, with his breath at my ear, Nick found my pleasure. I melted under his fingers, ready for all he had to give. As he touched me, he whispered words into my neck. I couldn't understand him, but I didn't care. His exquisite, teasing strokes drove me mad as he weaved magic, drawing me higher, then letting me fall before catching me again. As Nick worked, his tongue lazily circled my nipple, slowly, then faster, before he took it into his mouth.

I reached for him, desperate to pull him in, to feel all of him. But he stayed on task until I was a shivering wreck. With his fingers deep inside me, I threw my head back. "Please, now." Clawing at his chest, I was on the brink of exploding, and I wanted him along for the ride.

With a glorious grin, Nick moved on top, and, giving a low growl, buried himself inside me.

The pressure, the heat of him, was all I could focus on.

He moved slowly at first, each long, purposeful thrust stealing my breath... stealing my mind. With each stroke he kept pressure on the desperate bundle of nerves at my center, his thumb moving in the same pulsing, circular motion it had earlier. Under his touch, and his pounding rhythm, thunder rolled through my body.

The sensations he brought were like nothing I'd ever known. Pure bliss. I'd never abandoned myself to another person like this. But tonight, exquisite pleasure and the beautiful man moving above me consumed every fiber in my body. And I wanted to own every single, delicious moment.

I wrapped around his hips and with a grunt, Nick drove into me harder. His ragged breath grazed my ear as his body met mine, slick with perspiration. He'd shut his eyes as if he was in his own world. Was he thinking of someone else? Hell, I didn't care. All that mattered was his heat against me. Inside me. Over and over.

After what felt like hours, his circling thumb, the intense focus on his face, and the friction of skin against skin nudged me toward the edge. Bit by bit, tiny waves of euphoria engulfed me, as fingers of desire traced over my body, pulling me deeper into an ocean of exquisite pleasure. Lower and darker, drawing me into a bottomless expanse. The room closed in around me, and I teetered on the edge, letting out a long, throaty moan.

Hearing me, Nick opened his eyes, watching me with hunger. He said my name as he pushed even harder, even deeper.

Keeping a relentless rhythm, he drove me higher than I thought possible, until with his fingers at my center, and his hardness deep inside me, I came to a shuddering climax around him.

Only when I'd released my nails from his skin did he succumb to his own pleasure. With a gravelly growl, Nick buried his face in my neck, rocking into me over and over, until finally, we stilled together.

9

TATTOOS AND TENDERNESS

We laid exhausted, hot, and breathless, tangled on the blankets. The hammering of my heart fought with the rhythmic pull of Nick's chest. After a time, both settled, and he rolled away, removing his rubber, returning to lay next to me. He nestled his mouth into the crook of my neck, hot lips deliciously tickling behind my ear. I luxuriated against the warmth of his solid body pressed against mine.

"Well, that's me for another year," he murmured.

I smiled. Nick was still in Santa mode. "Thank you for your service."

He snickered against my neck. "I want you to know that I don't normally do this kind of thing."

I quirked a brow at him. "What sort of thing?"

He stroked my hair away from my forehead. "Corrupting beautiful women in hotel rooms on Christmas Eve. Hell, sometimes I don't see a woman for months."

I didn't know if he was still playing Santa or being honest about himself. I hoped for the latter. "We're both adults.

Besides, this might just go down as the most fulfilling Christmas *I* ever had."

He huffed another laugh against my skin, sending a shiver over my body. "There's nothing like spreading a bit of Christmas cheer."

As the snow fell silently outside the window, Nick moved to touch my hair, tangling and curling it between his fingers. His arm hovered centimeters from my eyes.

I reached up to trace the line of musical notes weaving around his bicep. "Your tattoos are beautiful." This close, I had the chance to inspect them. I ran my hand over flowers, trees, mountains and beautiful patterns that danced before my eyes. Almost his entire upper body was painted in ink.

"I didn't expect St. Nick to be quite so... I don't know... badass."

He laughed, the sound throaty, deep and delicious. "Badass?"

I pushed up on my elbow. "Look at you. The tattoos, the muscles. I don't recall ever seeing a greeting card like this." I ran my hand over his skin, settling on his chest.

Nick curled an arm around me, pulling me back down to meet his body. "There's a lot of months between my visits to town—a lot of solitude in Lapland. It gives me time to come up with new designs."

I grinned. "And work out. Tell me, does Mrs. Claus like to spot for you? Towel you down? I hope she appreciates your dedication."

Nick leaned to kiss the top of my head. "I don't go to the gym. And there's no Mrs. Claus. My elves made her up to deter groupies."

I gently batted my hand against him. He had to be kidding, right? "You said earlier that every one of your tattoos has a story. What's the most interesting? The most special?"

I lifted slightly on Nick's ribs as he sucked in a breath. With an exhale, he picked up my hand and placed my fingertips on his chest. Right over his left pec. "This one," he said, his voice deeper than ever.

I propped myself up, narrowing my eyes to see a small heart with an ornate "A" inside. My pulse didn't just skip a beat, it took off running and left me floating on air. "Nick! When did you get this?"

"Abbie," he said, shaking his head. "We're strangers, remember?"

The soft glow in his eyes sent a tingle of delight over me. I nodded and settled back down, laying my cheek on his skin. "What's the story behind this tattoo? Who was A?" My heart pounded as I waited for his response.

Nick shifted underneath me. "She was my best friend. The other half of me."

My gut tugged and I waited for him to say something else. Anything. After a long silence, I couldn't wait any longer.

"And what happened? Where is she now?"

He brought up a hand and pulled it through his hair. "She outgrew me. In the end, I don't think I was enough. But I can't blame her. She wanted bigger and better things than I could give her. But damn, I loved her."

With his words, a lump the size of a snow-globe formed in my throat. Nick held his breath beneath me, his body tight and still. I reached out, taking my hand and curling my fingers through his. After giving them the tiniest squeeze, I leaned in and placed a kiss on his tattoo. "I think your friend would love it. And I bet she'd like the chance to tell you that."

I let out a long yawn, blinking into the gloom of the room.

Nick chuckled and squeezed back against my hand, giving a slow shake of his head. "I wouldn't hold her to anything. But I do have a favor to ask *you* before I disappear."

He traced a pattern along my collarbone with a single finger. His touch had my body crying for more, but a heaviness settled over me. I yawned again and nuzzled into him. "Mmm?"

"Can I hold you while you fall asleep? I don't mean to sound creepy, but like I said, I don't see many women, and never one as beautiful as you."

In the crackled light of the fire I took a long breath, holding it in my throat. The thought of my oldest friend—my first love—holding me until I fell asleep had my heart aching and glowing in equal measure. Right now, I couldn't think of anything else I'd prefer. Tonight, we'd comfort each other. Tomorrow, we'd talk.

"If you don't mind seeing me drool on your pillow, I'd like that."

Nick's lips curled at my neck, his smile pressing into my skin. "I don't mind at all." With a sigh, he enveloped me in one muscular arm. With his free hand he brushed my hair away from my face. Finally, he pulled the blankets to cover us.

"You've no idea how much tonight meant to me," he whispered. "You were a wonderful Christmas present."

He leaned over and kissed me gently on the forehead, adding a tattoo of his own to my skin.

Nick continued to stroke my hair and under the gentle movement of his hand, I closed my eyes. The last thing I heard before a dreamy haze of sleep settled over me were his soft words in my ear.

"Merry Christmas, Abbie."

10

REGRETS AND REVELATIONS

My eyes fluttered open as I woke to unfamiliar sounds. The pulse at my temple thumped and the side of my butt ached. I brought my hand down to rub my hip and winced at the bolt of discomfort. Damn, I must have come down hard on it last night in the hallway. My whole body went rigid, and I tugged in a breath. Last night. The hallway. Nick!

I sat bolt upright in the bed, automatically reaching out to the dresser. With trembling fingers, I closed my hand around my glasses and put them on. My vision snapped into focus, and I knit my brows tight together.

I swept my gaze around the room. Just as I remembered, the fire sat across from the bed. It lay cold and gray, and the finest ash hung suspended in the shards of sunlight from the window. The old leather couch sat empty, and there was no jacket draped over its back.

Nibbling my bottom lip, I glanced at the empty bed beside me. All I saw were crinkled sheets, and silence filled the air.

Winter moths fluttered in my belly as I pulled my robe around me. I'd slept on it, and the warm cotton hugged my body just as Nick's arms had. I pushed off the bed and my feet dropped to the carpet. Where the hell was he?

Padding across the room, I found the door to the bathroom. The room layout was identical to my own. The only difference was the couch and the fireplace. Holding my breath, I leaned in, pressing my ear against the wooden panel straining to hear a sound from within. Nothing.

I poked at the door with my index finger, and it swung open, revealing empty space. My belly rolled. Just before I fell asleep, Nick said he'd disappear. I thought he was still playing Santa. But with the empty chill of the room, it felt like he'd never even been here.

A bitter taste rose in the back of my mouth. Who just ups and disappears after a night like we had? After we'd begun to build a bridge and reconnect?

I pushed into the bathroom and glared at my reflection in the mirror. A burn settled in my chest. My lips were red and swollen and Nick's beard had left a blotchy patina on my skin. With my unruly hair and eye bags—thanks Mom and familial genetics—I looked hideous. No wonder he'd run off.

As I splashed icy water on my face, all the tenderness and familiarity I'd felt with Nick fell away. As if I washed off every last trace of him. Sure, he'd called me beautiful and filled my heart with more hope than I'd had in years. But we'd made no promises. Formed no plans. Hell, we'd only talked as "strangers." I'd suggested the game, but my stomach churned at my foolishness.

I sighed. What did I expect? Even though we had history and danced together at The Timberline, I'd jumped into bed with him within an hour. A coldness crept through me, settling deep in my bones, and I couldn't shake the hollow gnawing at my chest.

Rubbing my throbbing temples, my gaze settled on my purse

laying on the side of the sink. I pulled up with a gasp. Hang on. Why was it here, in *this* bathroom? And come to think of it, I'd left my glasses on the nightstand back in my *own* room. But they'd been right by the side of the bed when I woke. I turned around to see my clothes neatly folded on the side of the bath.

The sound of excited voices outside the window broke through my galloping thoughts and I looked out to see a group of men shoveling snow from under the bus. My heartbeat quickened. They must've cleared the pass.

I brushed my teeth with the complimentary toothbrush, fixed my hair, and dressed, putting in the spare pair of contacts I always carried. Cissy and my folks would be so worried by now. They probably had no idea what happened to me and the thought of Mom fussing around the kitchen in a fluster made my chest ache.

Stepping back through the door, I ran my eyes over the empty room. Time to face reality, Abbie. My late-night encounter with Nick had been a dream. A fantasy. I'd taken full advantage of his kisses and pretty words, but now, I wanted to be back home as soon as possible. Safely away from the idea that Nick and I could ever be more than casual friends. I took one last look at the bed before picking up my bag and tramping out into the hallway.

~

In reception, I scanned the faces of the group of jostling people, searching for Nick. I don't know why I bothered. Nobody was tall. Nobody had rich hazel eyes, and nobody would be capable of making my heart thump like he could.

Instead, I spotted the red-cheeked lady I'd spoken to last night. She handed out pastries and steaming hot coffee to the guests.

Shifting from foot to foot, I mentally rehearsed what I'd say. Nick hadn't had a travel bag with him last night, so..

"Thanks for your hospitality. Have you seen a man in a red velvet suit?" didn't sound remotely sane. She'd think I'd gone nuts.

"Good morning, dear. Merry Christmas," she said, arriving at my side. "It looks like you'll be able to head out now. The road is clear."

I thanked her and took the offered croissant. The smell of the pastry filled my nose with its buttery sweetness.

"Let's go and sort your room payment," she said, putting down her tray and ushering me to the desk. "As mentioned last night, the charge won't be much, just a few dollars to cover electricity, cleaning and laundry, and anything you had from the minibar."

I swallowed, bracing myself for a heavy bill.

"What room did we give you?" As she spoke, she flipped index cards stacked neatly in a box.

I smiled. These small towns could be so old school. "Room 17, I think,"

The lady nodded and pulled out a card, cross-checking its information with a large book on the desk. She dragged one red tipped nail down the list of names and numbers, coming to a stop with a crisp tap to the page.

Her gaze flew up to mine, a tight smirk on her face. "It looks like someone's settled your bill already."

I shook my head. "No, I don't think so. I don't even have the key anymore. I ended up sleeping in..." My words trailed off.

The lady's eyes sparkled, and she threw me a conspiratorial grin. "Ah yes, that's right. In fact, I have something to give you."

She reached under the desk and handed me a plain white envelope. I took it with trembling fingers and turned away to open it. I held my breath as I tore into the thick paper. Inside was a small card bearing an old-fashioned picture of Santa Claus. With a breath in my throat, I read the message.

"Merry Christmas, Abbie. I know it's a lot to ask, but if you still want to talk, come down to St. Jude's, ward B. Love, St. Nick xo."

A breath hitched in my throat. Hazy memories of our magical night played in my mind again, and my skin tingled as I remembered the way Nick touched me, his tender words, and his delicious body. As I laid in his arms, my heart felt complete. Like I'd been put back together after being broken.

At the thought of his trusting eyes and his sweet smile, my heart thumped like a boxer working the pads. I turned back to the lady. "Can you tell me something, please? What is St Jude's?"

The lady's eyebrows lifted. "St. Jude's is the hospital in Pine Pass. Back down the hill. It's not far."

"Yeah, I know it," I said, my voice almost a whisper.

"The bus already made the journey once this morning."

My pulse skipped. "And the man who left this note, was he on it?"

The woman's face erupted into a grin. "What, Nick? Yes, he was. Such a gorgeous man, in more way than one." She wiggled her eyebrows at me. "You know, he dresses up as Santa every year for the children at the hospital." She leaned on the counter and folded her hands together under her chin, like she was about to teach me algebra or impart some ancient wisdom. "Keeps himself to himself mostly, but he's great with those kids. He got stuck on his way down there last night. He had to leave first thing. Needed to get there before the little ones woke up."

My skin tingled as warmth spread within my chest. Nick hadn't abandoned me. He hadn't left me high and dry. He had a good reason to leave, and it was all I could do to stop myself from bouncing around reception in my boots. I turned to the woman. "Thank you so much, and Merry Christmas."

She gave me a cheery wave as I picked up my bag. I stepped

out into the startling white snow and stood outside the front of the Pines Lodge.

As people hurried to load suitcases and bags into the waiting vehicles, chaotic thoughts filled my brain. Thoughts of Mom wringing her hands when she found my bed empty. Thoughts of Cissy trying to keep her calm. And thoughts of everything that had happened in the last twelve hours.

Thoughts of Nick and I… together.

I had to get to him. Tell him how amazing last night was, tell him *properly* how sorry I was for everything I'd done. Ask if we could still be friends… or maybe more.

I checked the clock on my phone. I had time. Christmas dinner wouldn't be on the table for hours.

The winter moths that'd earlier stirred in my belly took off this time, fluttering like a blizzard. Why shouldn't I take a chance on what Nick and I had? What we could be?

It was time to take my life back. Reach for what I really wanted. What I needed. Love and acceptance. And to stop letting other people keep me down.

With a deep breath and a leap of faith, I pulled on my hat and headed toward the bus descending the mountain.

11

ST. NICK AND SERENDIPITY

The hospital stood eerily quiet when I arrived. Nobody sat at the reception desk and no visitors waited in the hall. The only sounds were distant voices and squeals of laughter. The "whump" of my boots on the tiles echoed around the cavernous entryway, making me feel like an intruder.

Signage clearly wasn't a priority, so I followed the noise, like a trail of breadcrumbs. As I moved further into the building, the giggles and shrieks grew louder, and I smiled. Laughter and joy had been missing in my life recently, and it was good to hear.

As the noise swelled to a crescendo, a sign on the wall read, "Ward B, Pediatrics." With trembling hands, and blood roaring in my ears, I put down my bag and stepped around the corner.

In the center of the big room, surrounded by a gaggle of excited children, sat St. Nick. Santa Claus.

My Nick.

With his broad back to me, I recognized the strong curve of his shoulders, and the sandy blond hair tied into a ponytail at his nape. He let out a laugh as he scooped up a giggling child, propping them carefully into the seat next to him. The sound stole my heart.

I inched my way around the room at a snail's pace—heart in my throat. I ached to get a clear glimpse of his face.

Nick wore the same velvet suit, but this time he had on a red hat. Its fur trim gently hugged his forehead, and a large sleigh bell hung heavily on the end. As he moved his head, I heard the softest sound of jingling—the sound I heard last night, before I left my room. I smiled. If I hadn't heard it, I might never have ended up in the hallway under the laundry cart, needing rescuing.

Nick handed the child a present as I crept round the back of the room. The profile that greeted me today was crystal clear. In the light, with the help of my contacts, his beauty took my breath away.

I must've moved into his peripheral vision, because his eyes found mine like a sniper's bullet. A tight breath caught in my throat and my cheeks burned. There was no mistaking the warmth in his face, and the divine grin growing on his lips.

As if the years had peeled away, Nick smiled at me as he had a thousand times before. But this time was different. New emotions glowed in his eyes, causing buds of hope to bloom in my heart. I leaned against the wall to support my shaky legs. I didn't want to take his attention from the kids, so I sent him a little wave.

With a wink, Nick turned his attention back to the boy who opened his brightly wrapped present. There was no mistaking the kindness in his face—its familiar warmth. Warmth I'd often craved, lying alone after the angry words and rejection from my ex.

Regret weighed down on my chest like a boulder as I thought of the countless times I'd cursed myself for my actions at the Snowball all those years ago. The times I'd blamed myself for not going to find him. For not telling him how I really felt. How selfish and wrong I'd been.

After a few more minutes, a young girl unwrapped the last gift and had a final photo with Santa. Nick was alone now. When he stood and turned toward me, the look on his face made my heart backflip. The light in his eyes felt like the sun peeking out from behind a thick snow cloud. Like I was the only woman he ever wanted to see standing here against the wall.

Nick reached me, leaned in, laying a soft kiss on my cheek. "You came," was all he said.

"You got down here so fast."

He tipped his head to the side. "I had a head start. My reindeer are pretty fast."

A smile lit up his face, and I had an urge to kiss the dimple on his cheek.

"We shouldn't talk here," he said. "I don't want to shatter any of the kids' illusions. Can't have them thinking Santa's been playing the field."

I giggled, pushing a stray curl from my cheek. "Come on, surely even St. Nick has a romantic life. And you don't look anywhere near old enough to be the real Santa!"

"Well, right now, I'm on duty, so it's wholesome all the way for me."

I pointed my finger into the velvet of his solid chest. "Listen buddy! Last night was anything but wholesome."

He sucked in his lips and searched my eyes, as if he was reliving every single moment we had in the hotel room. Finally, he offered me his arm. I smiled, accepting his outstretched hand, and we walked back through the corridors and out into the cold together. As we met the crisp air, a light flurry of snow fell, and tiny flakes hung in the grey sky like stars.

I let go of his hand and wrapped my arms around my body as we walked. "Damn, it's cold. How do you stand it up here?"

Out of sight of the main entrance, Nick took off his velvet hat and placed it on my head. Its bell jingled crisply in the clear air. "We rely heavily on skin-to-skin contact," he said, drawing me toward him, warm hands on my arms. "I could always show you."

I looked into his eyes. Just like when we were kids, they were intense, startling even. But now they contained something else. Something new and just for us. But at the thought of our night, and this morning, my chest tightened.

"Why did you just leave me there, alone at the inn?"

A fine line scored between his brows, and he let out a long sigh. "I know how being left alone feels."

His words stung and my gut twisted. He meant in the same way I'd left him and gone to the Snowball with someone else. Left our friendship for something newer and more exciting.

"It feels pretty shitty," I muttered.

He shook his head, releasing my arms. "Look, I didn't do it to be cruel. I had to get down here fast, and you weren't waking up, so I left you. I'm sorry."

I clenched my jaw. I must have been completely out for the count. He probably departed a while before I woke, leaving only cold, crumpled sheets and a faint scent of cinnamon.

"I left the note to give you a choice, Abbie. I hoped you'd come and find me, and I hope now we can work out what last night was... what it meant." He took my hands, and his deep voice dripped over me like syrup on waffles. "I need to know if you meant what you said last night about loving me back then."

I let out a shaky exhale. "I can never change what I did... never take it back. But I want you to know that I loved you too. I just didn't realize how much." His face was unreadable, and my heart skipped like chipmunks on Red Bull. "I've wanted to tell you I was sorry for so long, but I never had the courage to do it. I wasted so much time."

Nick gave a slow nod. "Do you think you could feel the same way again?"

His voice was so breathy, so rich, that my insides curled in delight at the sound. I squeezed his hands. "I don't know if I ever stopped loving you, Nick. Certainly, nobody ever lived up to you. And last night? Last night was so perfect. We fit together. We always have."

Nick puffed the air out of his cheeks and soft pillows of condensation curled around us.

"I don't want to beg you to trust me again," I said. "But last night was amazing. I can't just walk away from that... or from you."

He reached out and took my hands, threading his fingers through mine. His hazel eyes roamed over my face, as if taking in each detail. Under his gaze, my mouth ran a little dry. I hoped he had a thing for shiny skin and two-day-old hair.

As if he read my mind, he spoke. "You're so beautiful. I can't believe you're here."

His words sent my heart soaring into the stratosphere. It beat like it would break out of my chest and bounce around right here in the gardens. I gazed up at him—at his smile. "I feel the same way. It's so good to see you, Nick."

After a beat, he bent down to give me a long, lingering kiss, his beard gently scratching my lips. I closed my eyes, lost in a million sensations and a million memories. We'd done so much together over the years—been so much together. And now, in the craziest way, we'd found each other again.

Nick curled his arms around my body and pulled me close. His heat crept through my jacket, and I wrapped my arms around him too. Our lips danced together as the snowflakes fell around us, but as voices reached our ears, he broke our kiss.

He didn't let me go, though. He held me close to his chest and I played with one of the gold buttons on his jacket. "How the hell did you get my stuff out of my room?"

He chuckled. "You were dead to the world. I know the hotel owner, so I got the spare key and carried it all over."

Had I drunk that much? With a flutter of the familiar moths in my belly, I recalled the line of bottles on the side of the bathtub. "Ugh. You must think I'm a degenerate."

Nick shook his head with a grin. "On the contrary. You're a gorgeous drunk. Very accommodating." He curled an eyebrow as he spoke, but then the playfulness left his face.

Nick looked down at his feet. Sensing he was about to move away from me, I held him tight. I wouldn't let him go this time. "What is it?"

His body tensed under my fingers. "I know I said I didn't want to talk about our past, but I think if we're going to have any chance of moving on, I need to lay it all out there."

I nodded, my breath shallowing by the nanosecond. Fine baby hair at Nick's temples fluttered in the breeze making him look like an angel. Like he wore a halo.

"I couldn't face you after the Snowball. I wasn't sure who you'd become. I didn't know what to say or if I trusted myself to say it."

I bit my lip, hot waves of guilt engulfing me.

"What you did was devastating. It broke me," he murmured. "I thought I meant more to you."

I closed my eyes, feeling the full weight of his words, knowing I could never take my actions back. After a long beat, I looked up at him again.

"I'm so very sorry. If only I could turn back time, things would be different. I know it's not enough to hear, but if I could go back, I would pick you. I would pick what we had. I want you to know that."

Nick stared into my eyes, as if trying to read the truth in them.

"Nothing I can say will ever change what I did. When you

disappeared, I felt like I'd lost my other half, too. Where did you go?" I asked.

He stayed silent, as if measuring his words. The snow fell heavier now, the flakes silently kissing the ground and kissing our clothes.

"I took off to stay with my Uncle Luke. I couldn't face town again. It would've meant seeing you with someone else and me being the butt of his jokes. And honestly, without you, there was no reason to stay."

Bitterness laced his voice, and I hung my head.

"Luke taught me to survive up there." He gestured to the mountains that loomed around us. "I love those woods and hills. My life is simple. I have my cabin, and I split trees for a living."

Well, that accounted for the muscles.

His beautiful mouth bowed upwards. "I found a kind of peace up there. I had a few girlfriends, broke some hearts, but there wasn't a day I didn't think about you."

My breath hitched and our eyes met. I felt the same way.

"Some days I cursed that you were born," he continued. "Some days I resolved to track you down. But most days, I just missed you. I'd rehearsed a thousand times what I'd say if I ever saw you again. And then last night, there you were, at my feet, covered in laundry and a little worse for wear."

His eyes creased at the corners. The tenderness in his gaze took my breath.

"And I couldn't even see you properly."

"But I could see you, Abbie. Crystal clear."

He curled his arms around me, breathing in the scent at my neck.

"And what did you see?" I asked.

"The *real* you. The old Abbie I'd lost."

"Old being the operative word," I said, shaking my head.

Nick smiled, running his eyes over my face before stopping

at my lips. “Even if you were gray and covered in wrinkles, I’d still want you.”

My breath retreated and without hesitation, I leaned in and kissed him. This kiss was different though—hungry and demanding—and he pressed his growing hardness up against me.

Damn. If this was life in the mountains, then I was sold.

“Hey! Santa!” A cry rang out in the courtyard as a group of older kids hung out of the hospital window, whistling and yelling at us.

“Is that Mrs. Claus?” the boy shouted.

Nick pulled away leaving me dizzy with longing.

“She’s hot!” the kid hollered, his friends nudging him, egging him on.

“Yes, she is,” Nick said quietly. His voice dripped with desire as his mouth drew close to my ear.

“And I’ve got some serious unwrapping to do before the day is out.”

THE END.

12

NUTCRACKERS AND NEW BEGINNINGS

I sprinkled icing sugar across the still warm cookies, tapping my palm against the metal sifter. Soaring notes from Nick's violin reached my ears through the kitchen door. I'd left him in the sitting room to play for Cissy and Harry's first dance.

We'd transformed the whole house into the winter wonderland my cousin wanted, and as I watched Nick play under the sparkle of fairy lights, my heart overflowed. I actually teared up.

He looked so beautiful—was so talented. And he'd watched me, too, with that special glow in his eyes. As the moisture threatened to spill over my lashes I had to leave. Better to get away before my makeup ran and I looked like a panda for the rest of the day.

I refilled the sifter before giving the cookies another pass. As I worked, the door creaked behind me. The sound of conversation and laughter increased, then faded again.

A sweet smell of cinnamon and pine reached me, and I smiled.

"I didn't think I'd find you here, wrist deep in baking." Nick's husky baritone swept over me.

I let out a breath. "What do you mean?"

I picked up the nutcracker on the counter and placed a hazelnut between its jaws. I wanted to sprinkle some of its shards over the cookies. With a grimace I squeezed the handles together.

Nick stepped up behind me. "Aren't you the bridesmaid? I thought your job was to fuss over your cousin all day."

I gave the hazelnut a second squeeze, and a tiny grunt escaped my lips.

Nick's chuckle wrapped around me, and he curled his arms around my waist. "Can I help you with that?"

I didn't like to admit defeat, but as I looked down at his corded, inked forearms, I wasn't about to refuse. He'd rolled up his shirt sleeves earlier. No smart wedding suit for my Nick. He was unapologetically himself, and I loved him for it.

I held my hands up like I'd surrendered to a bank robber, and he took the nutcracker from me before applying enough pressure with just one hand to crack the hazelnut like an egg.

"Thank you," I said, remembering Nick's powerful hands as he'd held me in place against his fridge only last night. I bit at my bottom lip.

"You're welcome. Someone has to clear your kitchen chores and get you back to the party. Cissy will notice you're not there."

I chuckled, handing him another nut to crack for me. "Are you kidding? Have you not seen how completely in love she and Harry are? I'd be lucky to get a word in between their kisses."

He cracked the nut then put it down on the counter along with the nutcracker. Within a heartbeat he brought his lips to my neck—his warm breath sending shivers down my spine.

"Seems like they have the right idea. Maybe we should join them."

My belly flipped in a full somersault, and I turned around in his arms to face him. "G-get married? I... I... we only just..."

Nick's hazel eyes flashed, and his now familiar throaty laugh filled the air between us. He shook his head. "Don't panic. I was thinking more of the kissing, but... if you like being back in Pine Springs and don't mind the snow, I wouldn't mind talking about it somewhere down the line. I can't imagine anyone else I'd rather hang out with for the rest of my days."

I swallowed hard, my breath rolling faster through my chest. His smile bowed even higher, and he brought his mouth to mine.

As we kissed, he circled my waist again, and I slid my hands over his chest, threading them around his neck. The feeling of the two of us together steadied my giddy heart. Nick couldn't imagine hanging out with anyone else for the rest of his days and I felt the same about being in his arms. Why did I ever stay away so long?

Savoring his lips, I sent a quick prayer of thanks to St. Medard, patron saint of blizzards. His timely intervention on Christmas Eve changed my life. If every snowstorm led to this kind of happiness, I'd gladly sign up for an extended stay at the North Pole.

Nick dragged one thumb down my arm, sending a shiver through my body. He'd done the same yesterday—again and again. After Nick and I left the hospital, I called Mom and explained why I wasn't home on Christmas morning. She started off the call getting herself into a tizzy, but the moment I mentioned Nick, she relaxed. With her approval, he took me to see his place in the mountains. We'd spent the rest of Christmas day eating doughnuts, drinking hot chocolate in front of the fire, and getting to know each other a whole lot better.

We'd talked late into the night. I agreed to stay in town a little longer. In fact, I wasn't sure I'd ever go back to California. As much as I loved the heat, with Nick in my life, there was more than enough sizzle in Pine Springs to keep me happy.

Nick ended our kiss. As our lips parted, he brought his hands to my shoulders and studied my face.

"What? Has my mascara run?"

"No. Hold still." Nick ran his thumb gently over my cheek then, with the sexiest smile known to womankind, brought it to his lips. He licked the tip. "Icing sugar."

I brought a hand to my face. "Oh, crap, am I covered in it? I probably look like a mess."

Nick raked his eyes over me, shaking his head. "Absolutely not. You look gorgeous. I don't think I've ever seen you look so charming."

At his words, a flash of heat ran through me, like I'd been struck by lightning. "Damn! I almost forgot to give you your Christmas present."

He huffed a soft laugh. "No, you didn't. I'm holding it. And it's perfect. Just what I always wanted."

Nick leaned in to kiss me again, but I held my hand to his chest. "No, I have something else for you." I dug into the hidden pocket in the side of my dress.

Nick widened his eyes. "You have pockets in there? I'm sorry, I assumed someone sewed you into that gown. You look incredible." He brought his mouth to my neck, trailing feather-light kisses behind my ear. With his touch, all thoughts of presents and Christmas left my brain, as my nerve endings sparked to life. Hell, he knew exactly how to distract me. But I had something that belonged to him. Something I wanted to return.

"Nick."

"Mmm?"

"We shouldn't. Someone could walk in."

He paused, lips hovering millimeters from my skin. “I have every faith in you.”

“Sorry, what?”

“I’m sure you could take an intruder down with those nutcrackers in a second.”

I giggled, drawing a small silk bag from my pocket. I took one of Nick’s hands and placed it in his palm. “Here, I wanted you to have this back.”

Nick examined the bag, quirking a brow. After a beat, he pulled open the drawstring and tipped out the contents. The music-note charm he’d given me, so many years ago, lay against his calloused palm. I’d kept it on the gold chain that belonged to my grandfather.

He flipped the charm over, running his finger over the metal. “Isn’t this...?”

I nodded. “I thought you might like it back. I hope you like it.”

The apples of his cheeks raised, and his eyes sparkled. “I love it. Thank you.”

Nick leaned in and gave me a lingering kiss on my forehead. “But what can I get you?”

Try a lifetime of watching him chop wood and keeping me warm at night. With a smile, I wrapped my arms around his waist. “You don’t need to get me anything.”

“Oh, I think I do.” Nick smiled and secured the charm around his neck.

“Well, you could book me in for a tattoo. One to match your special heart.”

His eyes sparked. “I don’t know, Abbie. A tattoo is pretty permanent.”

I grinned. “I’ll take my chances.”

He swept me up in his arms again, kissing me gently. “What kind of tattoo would you get?”

“I don’t know. Something to remind me of you.”

"Maybe an axe?"

My mind lingered on the memory of the wood splitting demonstration he'd given me yesterday at his cabin. I wasn't sure an axe was really my style, but I was more than ready to sit through a million wood-chopping lessons, should he require.

"How about a sleigh and reindeer across your back?" he asked.

I giggled. "That's a bit flashy for me."

His lips quirked at their corners. "Okay, maybe a little Santa hat or perhaps..."

"You know, I think I'm going to keep it simple."

He shook his head slowly. "You are anything but simple."

I tapped the back of my hand against his solid torso. "No, I mean simple, like us. As in we're simply meant to be together."

A broad smile spread over Nick's lips. "I can do simple. I love you, Abbie. I never stopped loving you and now that I have you back, I want to spend all my time loving you."

My breath hovered somewhere in the back of my throat. If the last forty-eight hours were any measure, I wanted him to spend all his time loving me, too.

I cupped Nick's face, tracing his cheekbones with my thumbs. "I love you too—so much. I still can't believe everything that's happened, but I've got Ms. Carey, my loose beanie, and my shocking balance skills to thank for it. And this Christmas? Hands down the best."

With a lift of his brow and a grin that stole my breath, Nick leaned in. The moment we kissed, his hands wrapped around my back, and a wave of excitement flooded through me, electric and undeniable. He held me close, and in that moment, all my dreams had come true. My first love and I had found our way back to each other. Our *hearts* had found their way back to each other.

We had a second chance. An opportunity to start again.

And with St. Nick driving our sleigh, I couldn't wait to see where our journey would take us.

KEEP IN TOUCH!

Are you curious to discover more of my books? Sign up to my newsletter at:

https://terrific-bread-223.myflodesk.com/366011b5-e71d-4cbd-b23d-60f574c829df

and I'll send you a free steamy rom-com.

Power Moves is the starter book for the Tales from Tottenbridge Series.

This cheeky, slow-burn tale will leave you smiling and tingling in all the right places!

DID YOU ENJOY ST. NICK?

Why not leave a review!

Reviews are an indie author's best tool for reaching new readers, and loyal readers like you make all the difference. If you enjoyed this story, I'd love it if you could take a moment to share what you liked. It doesn't have to be long, but it'll make my day!

https://books2read.com/u/4AMXDd

Thank you in advance xxx

START YOUR VICKI HILTON JOURNEY HERE:

A Country Quandary

Book One in the Tales from Tottenbridge Series.

From high-powered lawyer to high-maintenance farm hand in 48 hours. What can go wrong?

Join Kitty's hilarious journey from job loss to farm life! She's a neat freak in a world of mud and mayhem, torn between a sexy playboy and a charming vet. Will she choose love in the country or cut her losses and return to the city? One thing's for sure, it's a summer Kitty will never forget.

https://books2read.com/u/3nNBJo

A LITTLE ABOUT ME!

Writing about love, passion and all things swoony has always been my dream. Originally from rural England, I now live in Sydney's glorious Northern Beaches, where I'm steadily gathering freckles and dipping my toes into the ocean for inspiration.

I create steamy, slow burn, contemporary romance with a focus on smart, quirky heroines and sensitive, sexy heroes. My books are always on the funny side, with a nice touch of spice.

I'm a devoted wife, mother of one beautiful daughter, a wrangler of assorted animals, and a lover of Skittles. It's a mix made in heaven.

If this book made you smile and filled your heart with a little joy, then I've done my job.

Come and find me at:

https://Vickihilton.com

https://www.facebook.com/groups/1455751891853556/

FINAL ACKNOWLEDGMENTS

Thank you to Mr. Hilton. You had no idea you married a writer, and your tolerance for our perpetually untidy house and the incessant tapping of my keyboard knows no bounds. I love you.

To my daughter, who stoically spends hours at a time, listening to my ramblings about plots and characters; I am so grateful. Your patience and love of storytelling warms my heart.

A big shout-out to my amazing ARC and street team. That you are happy to invest your time reading my stories blows me away. Getting to know you has been incredible and I'm so honoured to have such an awesome bookish family.

Last, but certainly not least, thank you to my amazing editor. Heather at Write-On Studios. You keep me sane, provide me with a lot of giggles, guinea pig and pug pics, and above all, make me look good! I never worry about my work when it's in your hands. Our shared love of commas is a thing of glory!

Thank you.

Created with Vellum

Printed in Great Britain
by Amazon

51908637R00056